"I'll take responsibility for this," Roxane said.

"We both will."

Zito looked briefly dangerous. "If you think that I'm going to hand you money and leave you to it," he said, "think again. You must know this changes everything."

Her small laugh was slightly hysterical. "You don't need to tell me that!" Already her life was in the process of turning upside down.

"You can't be left on your own."

"I've been on my own for over a year! I won't be the first single mother."

"You're not a single mother! This child has a father." With deceptive quiet, Zito added, "I won't leave you to fend for yourself while you carry my child."

EXPECTING!

She's sexy,
successful...
and
PREGNANT!

Relax and enjoy our fabulous series
about couples whose passion results in
pregnancies...sometimes unexpected! Of course,
the birth of a baby is always a joyful event, and
we can guarantee that our characters will
become dedicated parents—but what happens
in those nine months before?

Share the surprises, emotions, drama
and suspense as our parents-to-be come
to terms with their new babies. All will
discover that the business of making babies
brings with it the most special love of all....

Celebrate our new arrival,
The Riccioni Pregnancy
Daphne Clair

Daphne Clair

THE RICCIONI PREGNANCY

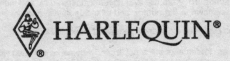

EXPECTING!

She's sexy, successful... and PREGNANT!

◆ HARLEQUIN®

TORONTO • NEW YORK • LONDON
AMSTERDAM • PARIS • SYDNEY • HAMBURG
STOCKHOLM • ATHENS • TOKYO • MILAN • MADRID
PRAGUE • WARSAW • BUDAPEST • AUCKLAND

Readers are invited to visit Daphne Clair's Web site at:
http://www.daphneclair.com

ISBN 0-373-12305-1

THE RICCIONI PREGNANCY

First North American Publication 2003.

Copyright © 2002 by Daphne Clair de Jong.

CHAPTER ONE

SHE was being followed. Silently, invisibly, but the prickling sensation at her nape and between her shoulder blades gave a primeval warning. Behind her the night hid a hunter.

She had walked down this narrow, sloping street hundreds of times, in daylight and darkness, and never been nervous. Until now.

The street lamps were obscured by trees that lined the narrow verge and cast deep shadows, wayward roots making treacherous humps and cracks underfoot. She should have changed her shoes before leaving work. The heels of her navy courts were high enough to be dangerous in the dark.

She tripped, let out a whispered exclamation, and cast a hurried glance over her shoulder, her heart accelerating.

Nothing. But it would be easy for anyone who didn't want to be seen to dodge behind a tree or one of the parked vehicles along the street. Few of the houses had room for a garage. They'd been built huddled cosily together before the motor car became a way of life.

Instinct quickened her pace, one hand fumbling for a key in the bag that swung from her shoulder.

At her neighbour's gate she paused, casting another glance behind her. Was the moving shadow under one of the trees a trick of the faint night breeze stirring the leaves in the inadequate lighting, or…?

Briefly she pictured herself pounding on the door, pleading for entry, saw the cheerful, phlegmatic Tongan family taking her in, sending out their muscular menfolk to deal with the lurking stranger. But no lights showed, no sound of the teenagers' music videos or the adults' rich, rapid voices floated into the street.

And what if she was mistaken? Fleeing some phantom attacker who didn't exist?

Her own gate was only yards away, and the safety of her home, the two-storey cottage that recalled New Zealand's colonial past.

Don't run. A few quick strides, a practised fumble with the latch and then she was on the short brick pathway, the gate clanging shut behind her, the drooping leaves of the kowhai brushing the shoulders of her suit as her fingers closed at last on the key in her bag.

She was on the second of the three worn wooden steps to the tiny porch when the gate clanged again, and she whirled, backing up the last step as a tall male figure materialised, closing on her.

One high heel caught in a gap between the worn boards, and she lost her balance, flinging out a hand to steady herself and losing her grip on the key.

She grabbed at a painted post, heard the key clatter to the brick path, saw the dark bulk of the man's wide shoulders as he stooped and picked it up.

There was no way she could get past him. She was trapped with a locked door behind her. And before her, a man with her key in his hand, already straightening.

She lifted her head, opened her mouth, drawing breath into her lungs ready to scream and hope someone would hear—someone who would help.

He took the steps in one stride, and a large, warm hand clamped over her mouth, strangling the sound at birth.

Smartly, viciously, she lifted her knee, but he was already behind her. She tried to bite, her teeth finding no purchase against the broad, suffocating palm. She kicked backward with a lethal heel but he was obviously prepared for the ploy and she found only empty air. Her elbow, aimed for his solar plexus, was caught in a hard hand that slid to her wrist, then his arm went around her, bringing her against an equally hard masculine body.

Then his breath was in her ear, his voice low, harsh. 'Darling, don't.'

Darling? Her whole body went rigid within the iron circle of his arm across her midriff.

Darling? Fury replaced fear.

Her temples throbbed as if her heart were sending all her blood there, and her limbs went hot and boneless. His imprisoning embrace slackened a fraction, and she used the moment to twist away and face him, her right hand swinging up with all her weight behind it, delivering a slap that resounded in the quiet street like a gunshot, the force of it almost rocking him off his feet.

'Bastard!' Her voice was shrill and wavering and she wished she'd kept her mouth shut. Now he knew she was panicked, a hysterical woman shrieking futile insults because she'd been frightened out of her mind by a man looming from the night.

His face was invisible in the darkness but she saw him lift a hand, and in a blind, useless attempt at avoidance she retreated the few inches that were left to her before her back collided with the locked door.

And then he laughed.

She heaved air into her lungs. Her head was buzzing and she seemed to be floating somewhere in space—dark, disorienting space. She had to take another breath before she could speak. Gritting her teeth, making her voice hard and steady, she said, 'Give me my key.'

He held it out to her, waiting for her to take it.

She snatched at it, but for a fraught moment he didn't release it, and her fingers were touching his.

Adrenalin raced from her fingertips and through her body, making it weightless, every nerve humming with electricity. Then he relinquished the key and she whirled and tried to fit it into the lock, unable to find the tiny slot because she was shaking so badly.

Strong male fingers closed over hers, and she jumped, then he was taking the key, efficiently inserting it, turning it, his hand on her back as he opened the door and thrust her ahead of him.

Now they were both inside and he'd shut them into a deeper darkness, together. Her eyes useless, her other senses at screaming pitch, she could hear the faint sound of his strangely uneven breathing, smell clean cotton and wool, soap and a hint of something woodsy—and underneath it the long-unfamiliar, earthy and shockingly seductive scent of male arousal.

His hand was still at her waist, and his arm came further about her, pulling her to him. 'You're trembling,' he said. Her temple was grazed by the subtle rasp of a shaven chin. 'I'm sorry.'

'So you bloody should be!' Anger was a defence against shame and confusion. She wrenched away from him, reached blindly for the light switch and blinked in the sudden cruel glare at watchful burnt-sienna eyes, black brows drawn together in a frown above a masterful nose, and a mouth fixed in a taut line that failed to hide its sensuous masculinity.

His eyelids lowered as he studied her face in return. 'You're pale,' he told her.

She felt pale. 'Have you been stalking me?' she demanded.

The upward jerk of his head dislodged a strand from the severely combed sleekness of salon-styled night-black hair. 'Stalking?'

'You were following me. Don't tell me you weren't trying to hide.'

'I was trying not to frighten you.'

She almost laughed. 'You *what?*'

'I thought if you saw—or heard—a man behind you in this lonely street you'd have reason to feel afraid.'

'So what the hell did you think I'd feel, knowing someone was there and deliberately keeping out of sight?' Agitatedly she slipped the bag from her shoulder, dumping it next to the phone on the half-round table near the door.

'I didn't think you knew.'

He reached out and took her hand, placing the key into the palm and closing the fingers over it. And then he bent his head and pressed his lips briefly to the fine skin of her inner wrist, sending the pulse wild and making her tremble even more.

Immediately he lifted his head, and even as she tried to tug away he scanned her face again, his eyes far too prescient. 'You need a drink,' he said.

He looked about them and saw the door to her living room behind him, the furniture dimly discernible. Before she knew it he was drawing her into the room, switching on the light. She made another effort to pull away but he took no notice. 'Sit down,' he ordered, guiding her to the couch set at right angles to the small fireplace, with a solid, beautifully-grained pale rimu coffee table before it.

She sat down because she still felt as if her bones had deserted her. 'I don't need a drink, and if I did I'm quite capable of getting it myself.'

His withering look said he didn't believe either claim. He swept a hawkish gaze about the room, and went to the glass-doored corner cabinet where a half dozen bottles occupied one shelf and a neat array of tumblers and goblets another.

Knowing he would ignore any further protest, she tightened her lips and waited until he came back with amber liquid in a squat crystal tumbler and handed it to her.

She gulped half of the brandy, making her throat burn, and her eyes water so that involuntarily she closed them.

The seat cushions beside her depressed, and she opened her eyes and stiffly turned her head.

One long arm resting on the back of the couch, he watched colour burn into her cheeks. The brandy, she told herself. She wished he wouldn't sit so close— his thigh, encased in well-pressed dark pants that matched his superbly cut jacket, almost touching hers where the skirt of her lightweight suit bared her knees.

'Drink it all,' he said.

She should tell him to go to hell, that she didn't want him or any man pushing uninvited into her home, ordering her about and deciding what she needed. It wasn't hard to guess what he thought she needed...

Lifting the tumbler, she emptied it. Dutch courage. Her hand stayed clenched about the cool, delicate glass; a wonder that it didn't break.

He said, 'Do you live alone here?'

'That's none of your business.' The answer snapped out before she'd thought.

Damn. Why hadn't she claimed a boyfriend—a big, burly, protective boyfriend? Or a half dozen flat-mates, due home at any moment. Although the cottage wasn't big enough for that many, with only two bedrooms. 'How long have you been following me?' she asked.

'I saw you get off the bus in Ponsonby Road. Do you often walk home alone in the dark?' He sounded condemnatory.

Ponsonby Road was popular for its eclectic mix of businesses, where homesick Pacific Island immi-grants could buy taro and yams, pawpaw and bread-fruit, and Fijian Indian women their jewel-coloured saris in tiny, crammed shops cheek by jowl with airy galleries of trendy local and imported art. But the long, busy road was best known for its restaurants and sidewalk cafés. Crowded and well lit, it was only a few hundred yards uphill from the cottage.

She said, 'I've always been perfectly safe until tonight.'

'You were safe tonight. I made sure of that.'

'Thank you for your concern,' not concealing her sarcasm, 'but it was unnecessary.'

'Once I had seen you it was totally necessary,' he contradicted her. 'Do you mind if I pour myself a drink?'

'Yes. I do mind.'

Black brows silently rose. The slightest flicker of his eyelids conveyed displeasure. 'So rude?'

Stupidly, she felt reproved. As if he had a right to scold her for bad manners.

He looked at her for a moment or two, then without haste rose and went back to the cabinet, where with some deliberation he poured vodka into another glass. 'Anything more for you?' he inquired with equally deliberate courtesy.

Seethingly silent, she shook her head, and he returned to her side.

Damn him, he knew she couldn't bodily throw him out. He was establishing his physical superiority, claiming territory. But this was *her* territory, and he was an intruder.

Looking down at the vodka without drinking, he said softly, 'You surely don't expect me to walk away now?'

If only. But she owed it to herself to try. 'Would you,' she inquired baldly, 'if I asked you to?'

He was still staring into the depths of his glass. The liquid didn't move—his hands were perfectly steady. Unlike hers. Her whole body was racked with tiny, invisible tremors. It was a moment before he said, 'Are you asking?'

She stopped breathing. She was sure she could hear her heart beating, slow and heavy, and her throat was locked.

Say it. 'Yes.'

She'd said it, not as decisively as she'd have liked to, but clearly enough, even if her voice was low in her throat.

Seconds ticked by. Then he lifted the glass and swallowed, lowered it again, holding it in both hands. He turned his head and she received the full force of the ferocious blaze in his eyes, so that she recoiled, her lower lip briefly caught in her teeth.

'No,' he said.

She shot to her feet, then halted because the sudden movement had made her a little dizzy—the damned brandy again—and besides, where was there to run to? He could corner her easily before she'd taken half a dozen steps.

As if to confirm it, he downed the remainder of his drink and stood up too, leaving the glass on the carpet by the couch. 'No,' he repeated. 'You can't run from me any more, Roxane.'

CHAPTER TWO

'I'M NOT running.' It made her sound as if she'd fled without thought, in blind fear. The room tilted, and she hastily sat down again. 'I've never *run* from you.'

'What would you call it, then?' he demanded.

'It was a decision. A rational, sensible decision.'

His lip curled. 'Rational? Sensible?'

A sensation sickening in its familiarity washed over Roxane. Helplessness, despair, and mingled with it a deep, inexpressible longing. 'You don't think I'm capable of that. But it was the best decision of my life.'

His jaw tightened and a small muscle in his cheek kicked almost invisibly. The anger that still smouldered in his eyes turned bleak before thick black lashes hid them. 'Was it necessary,' he asked bitingly, 'to be so dramatic—cutting off all contact, swearing your parents to secrecy, making me communicate through your lawyer as if I were some brute who had beaten you?'

'I told him you hadn't,' she said swiftly, looking down at her hands, wound tightly into each other. The solicitor had jumped to obvious conclusions, and she'd made sure he didn't retain them. 'You're not a brute, Zito.'

'God—' he breathed the word as if it rasped his

14

throat '—I thought I'd never hear you say my name again.'

Roxane winced, thankful that her head was still bent and he couldn't see her face, shadowed by the shoulder-length sable fall of her hair. But the change in his voice forced her to look up, her clear green eyes wondering.

To find his expression rigid and unreadable, his gaze cool, almost indifferent. 'Did it occur to you that if I wanted you back I could have found you?'

'I know you could have.' She tried to ignore the gibe in his caveat, *if I wanted you*... Zito could afford to pay any number of private detectives, for as long as it took.

'You'd made it clear you didn't want to be found.' He paused, a corner of his mouth curving satirically. 'Or were you hoping that I'd somehow do it anyway and come running after you, begging you to return to me?'

Sometimes, weakly, she had fantasised that he would track her down regardless of her efforts, that he'd come to her with apologies and promises and a new understanding—a changed and humbled man, and everything would miraculously be all right. There had been long cold nights when the fantasy had helped her through to another dawn.

But it would be fatal to admit it. 'No!'

She thought she saw a brief flare of some emotion—frustration? disappointment?—before he resumed the guarded watchfulness he'd shown earlier. She must have been mistaken, falling prey to all-too-familiar wishful thinking. 'I'm glad you didn't,' she said.

He swung away from her, pushing back the jacket of the perfectly tailored suit by shoving his hands into the pockets of his trousers.

Zito's clothes had always been impeccable, discreetly expensive but worn with an insouciance that made them part of the man, not any kind of status symbol to impress others.

Now he was inspecting the walls that she'd painted palest jade green and hung with cheap reproduced art, along with a couple of originals by local unknowns.

His gaze next disdained the calico covers hiding the shabbiness of her comfortable secondhand couch and the mismatched armchairs facing it across the low table that bore the honourable scars of a chequered life. For a few seconds his attention was caught by the worn, silky antique rug that Roxane had spent too much on but loved all the more for it.

He swept another sharp-eyed glance about the room, before he turned to her.

Roxane asked defiantly, 'Don't you like it?'

He didn't answer immediately, and when he did his voice was expressionless. 'It's very attractive. Small but…cosy.'

'I like small.'

For a moment the wicked, teasing sexual humour that had attracted and excited and confounded her when they first met gleamed in his eyes, lifting one eyebrow and a corner of his mouth in subtle disbelief. And damn, she responded to it as always, with a frightening mix of inward laughter and sheer wanton, bone-melting desire.

Keeping her expression blank, she hoped her eyes wouldn't betray her.

The laughter died and his mouth went hard. To her considerable surprise, he looked away first. 'Is the house yours?' he asked, almost as if it were a random question plucked from the air.

'Mine and the bank's.'

Her stock answer, but she should have expected the sudden stabbing quality of his stare. 'If you needed money you could have asked me. Through your lawyer if necessary. I told him—'

'I don't want your money. I have a good job and I can afford the mortgage.'

'Mortgage!'

He made it sound like a dirty word. Roxane smiled thinly. 'It's what we little people have when we need to buy a house.'

'You have no need to buy a house. I can give you anything you need—hell, I *did* give you everything!'

'Not everything,' she said softly, sadly. Not the one thing she needed above all.

Furious, he said, 'I loved you!'

She wouldn't even think about what that past tense meant. 'I know. I know you did. In your own way.'

He thrust a hand savagely over his hair, the frown turning to a scowl. 'I gave you my heart and my soul, everything that was in me. I don't know any other way.'

Of course he didn't. Maurizio Riccioni never had done a thing in his life except in his own inimitable, confident, and usually hugely successful way. Why should he have ever imagined that his marriage, his wife, might not succumb to that combination of self-assured charm and incisive decision-making?

Almost compassionately she said, 'It wasn't all your fault. I was too young, and I should have said no when you asked me to marry you.'

'You did,' he reminded her.

Yes, she had, the first time he asked her, showing a shred of common sense. But her opposition hadn't lasted long. She'd soon had her fears and scruples overturned one by one under the onslaught of Zito's clever brain, unswerving will, and devastating kisses. He had even talked her parents round, despite their misgivings about their only daughter marrying at nineteen.

He'd reluctantly waited until she turned twenty, and on her birthday she'd stood beside him while they exchanged their solemn vows in the cathedral in Melbourne, with all the trimmings and before several hundred guests.

But marriage was more than a frothy white dress and a champagne reception. And theirs hadn't stood the test.

'I should have stuck to my refusal,' she admitted.

'Thank you.' His voice held an acrid note. 'Sometimes I wish I *had* beaten you.'

'Zito!'

He managed to look both shame-faced and impatient. 'You know I'd never hurt you, or any woman! But it would give me a reason for your desertion—something that made sense.'

He started prowling round the room again, stopping at the small desk that she'd found in one of the few remaining Ponsonby junk shops that didn't have pretensions to being an antique store. When she'd sanded and polished it the grain of the timber had come up nicely.

Zito took a hand from his pocket and idly shifted aside a 'personal invitation' to subscribe to a book club at a 'once-only' price, revealing the envelope underneath.

'Those are private!' Not that she had anything in particular to hide. There was only more junk mail, bills and a letter from a cousin in England.

He looked at her unseeingly, his finger stilled on the sheet of paper, then lifted his hand, looking down again. Finally he turned fully. 'Ms Roxane Fabian?'

Why did she feel guilty? Roxane shrugged.

'You told me you were happy to take my name,' he said, his voice thickening, 'when we got married.'

'I didn't mind…it was no big deal.'

'It was to me. A very big deal.'

Just as reverting to her maiden name had become important for her. She supposed it was symbolic. 'An ownership thing?' she accused, trying for mild amusement.

He controlled his temper, covering it with a hard laugh. 'If you thought that, then you *were* too young.'

Or too stupid, his tone implied. '*You* didn't think so…then.'

His reaction was barely noticeable, but Roxane was so attuned to his every tiny movement she saw the stiffening of his muscles, the infinitesimal recoil. She'd pierced the armour of his self-confidence, however minutely.

The elation she felt disconcerted her. She had

never deliberately set out to wound Zito. Of course she'd known he would be upset and angry when she left him, but she'd had no thought of revenge or punishment, only a dire need for self-preservation.

In her long and probably incoherent farewell letter she had assured him that she didn't hate him, and he shouldn't blame himself for what he couldn't help. She had tried not to hurt him any more than the simple fact of her departure inevitably would.

Maybe the hurt had gone deeper than she'd expected. He'd had more than twelve months to get over it, but his jabbing little remarks weren't accidental.

'I'm sorry,' she said. 'I suppose it was too much to expect you'd understand.'

'Was there another man?' he asked abruptly. And looked around again, as if searching for evidence. 'Have you left him too?'

Roxane's temper snapped. 'Oh, for God's sake!' He couldn't conceive that she'd just wanted to be alone, that she could manage on her own? 'Another man, after living with you for nearly three years?'

At her scorching tone he looked arrested, almost confused. She added, 'And how *dare* you suggest I was unfaithful?'

Her anger seemed to give him pause. He shot a look at her from under his brows. 'For months I tortured myself with the thought...'

It hadn't even occurred to Roxane that he would think that. How could he have...? This was further proof that he'd never really known her, never bothered to comprehend her deepest needs. A small ache shifted from somewhere near her heart and lodged in her throat, stifling her voice. 'You were wrong.'

A lifting of his shoulder, a tilt of his head, seemed to indicate it was not important. But of course it was. His pride would have suffered, and he had a surfeit of that. If the truth were known, pride was probably the real reason he had refrained from sending someone looking for her, rather than respect for her stated wishes.

'You broke your other marriage vows,' he said. 'Why not that one?'

'It's different!'

'How?'

The question was unanswerable. 'Anyway, you were wrong,' she reiterated.

He gave her a piercing stare, and nodded as if accepting that. 'And now?' he inquired softly.

'Now?' About to snap a hot rejoinder, Roxane paused, her chin lifting. 'Now my private life is my own.'

His eyes narrowed, and she had to resist an instinct to let hers skitter away.

A shrill burring made her jump, and she said foolishly, 'That's my phone.'

Careful not to rise too hurriedly this time, she went to the hallway to lift the receiver. 'Yes?'

Zito stood regarding her through the open door while she tried to give her attention to the caller. 'Yes, Leon.'

Wrenching her gaze from Zito's inimical stare, at the corner of her eye she saw him swing round and disappear from her line of sight.

'Saturday?' Roxane forced herself to concentrate. 'Yes, it *is* short notice. Wait while I get my diary.'

She dug it from the bag she'd left by the phone. 'You do mean Saturday next week? What kind of party? If it's black tie formal...'

Leon assured her it wasn't. An impromptu welcome home, he said, for a son returning from overseas with his new fiancée. 'A family affair. About a hundred guests.'

'Just an intimate little gathering?' Roxane felt sorry for the unknown young woman. 'So the relatives get to cast their eyes over the bride-to-be?'

'It could lead to more introductions. These people are some of Auckland's best-known socialites. I hope you're free to supervise as well as make the arrangements?'

Roxane's own social life was low-key and intermittent. 'I'll be there on the night,' she promised.

'I know I can rely on you.'

Silly to feel a glow of satisfaction at the banal words, but when she returned to the little sitting room after hanging up, her lips were curved in pleasure.

Zito was standing at the long old-fashioned window. He faced her as she paused inside the door, and his eyes didn't match his casual tone when he spoke. 'Boyfriend?'

She didn't have a boyfriend, but the suggestion made her hesitate before answering. 'Business.'

'Business?' he repeated sceptically. 'At this time of night?'

'It's not that late.' She checked her watch. Just after nine.

Zito brushed that aside. 'Saturday night—a party?

An *intimate* party. Did you really need to consult your diary, or was that just to keep him on his toes?'

'You're being absurd.'

He came away from the window. His eyes were obsidian, glowing with a dark fire, his high cheekbones outlined with dusky colour under his natural tan. 'Absurd, am I?'

'Yes!'

Maybe it was the fierce contempt in her tone that stopped him, just a few feet from her. Certainly it was the first time she'd ever stood up to him like this.

'So who is this bride-to-be?' he shot at her. 'You? Because if so, you've forgotten a small detail, haven't you?'

Roxane was so astonished she laughed.

And saw again, with a surge of strange triumph, that she'd unsettled him. She had never seen Zito wrongfooted so many times in the space of—what? Half an hour?

It was a peculiarly heady sensation.

Tempted to let him retain his hasty assumptions, she decided that would be unnecessarily childish. Crisply, she informed him, 'That was my boss. We organise and cater events, mostly for corporates and big business, but he was asking me to make the arrangements for a private welcome home and engagement party for a client's son.'

Zito stared at her as if trying to decide whether she was telling the truth, then he sank abruptly onto the nearby couch and bowed his head, his fingers combing through the black strands, and muttered something she couldn't catch.

After a small hesitation Roxane sat in one of the armchairs facing him. Knees and ankles pressed together, she folded her hands in her lap. Capable hands, the nails allowed to grow just over the tips, and glossed with clear satin polish. Ringless hands. Hastily she covered the left one with her right.

When she looked up Zito was leaning against the couch cushions, looking disgruntled, his long legs sprawled in front of him. 'I've been stupid tonight,' he said unexpectedly. 'Clumsy and stupid.'

Startled by the admission, Roxane didn't argue, regarding him warily.

His eyelids drooped as his gaze lowered to her mouth, and then without haste traversed her body, making her skin prickle pleasurably in reluctant response. 'I should have caught up and stopped you after you got off that bus,' he said.

'Instead of scaring me witless?'

'When did you know it was me?'

When he'd called her 'darling' in his unforgettable, dark-melted-chocolate-and-brandy voice, that she'd always imagined held a trace of his Italian ancestry, although he was a second-generation Australian.

'Just before I hit you,' she told him.

He laughed. She remembered that he'd laughed then too, although the slap must have hurt.

Old emotions stirred, treacherously. Against the quickening in her blood she curled her hands, gripping one inside the other.

To quell the memories she said, 'What were you doing in Ponsonby Road, anyway? For that matter, what are you doing in Auckland?'

'We're thinking of opening a New Zealand branch of Deloras. I was dining at GPK.'

'Checking out the possible competition?' Zito's grandfather had arrived in Australia as a penniless assisted immigrant, and worked as a dishwasher and kitchen hand until he opened his own small restaurant, and then another, and another. Over the years the family business had become a multi-million dollar Australian institution.

And now they were planning to expand across the Tasman Sea and conquer the New Zealand market?

'Combining business with...pleasure,' Zito said.

Her skin tightened. 'You were with a woman.'

Of course he hadn't been eating alone. And of course his companion had been female.

'A woman I won't be seeing again.'

'I'm not surprised, if you left her flat in the middle of a meal.' The waspishness of her voice was simply on account of his unusual lapse of manners, Roxane assured herself. She had no right to be jealous. And of course she wasn't. 'What on earth did you say to her?'

'I apologised, gave her some money for the meal and a taxi, and said I'd phone her in the morning.'

Poor woman. Roxane very nearly laughed. 'You'll be lucky if she accepts the call.'

'I'll send her some flowers,' he said dismissively.

'Oh, that's sure to bring her round.' That and his notoriously irresistible charm. 'You'll have her eating out of your hand in no time.'

She'd irritated him. 'As a gesture of apology,' he said. 'I told you I won't be seeing her again. She's a casual acquaintance—nothing more.'

Who had probably hoped to be much more. The woman would never know what a lucky escape she'd had.

Roxane knew she was being unfair. An older, more sophisticated woman, more sure of herself than Roxane had been when she married Zito might have been perfectly happy—and made him happy too. She took a deep breath, blinked fiercely and stared at a blank spot on the wall.

'What's wrong, Roxane?'

Strangely, he sounded as if he really cared about the answer. Roxane blinked again and made herself look at him, saying the first thing that came into her head. 'I haven't eaten since lunch. I'm hungry.'

The remark must have spilled out of her subconscious, perhaps triggered by his talk of an abandoned dinner.

And for some reason it seemed to make him angry again. 'Will you never learn to look after yourself?' he asked.

'I have,' she replied icily. 'If you hadn't attacked me and dragged me in here and poured brandy down my throat, I'd have had something to eat by now.'

That was probably half the reason for her sluggish light-headedness—shock followed by alcohol on an empty stomach.

'I can fix that.' He got up. 'Where's your kitchen?'

'What?'

'Never mind.' He was already leaving the room. 'I'll find it.'

'Zito...' She stood up too, following after him while he strode along the short passageway and unerringly found the kitchen at the back of the house.

'Zito,' she repeated as he switched on the light, 'I don't need you to *fix* anything for me.'

He turned and gave her his most dazzling smile. Generations of charismatic Italian genes had produced that smile.

Taking her arm, he drew her to the small round table in the window corner, pulled out one of the aqua blue spray-painted wooden chairs and planted her on the cheerful patterned seat cushion. 'I'm still hungry too. And there's no reason you should have to cook for me. Just sit there and tell me where everything is.'

He slipped his coat and tie off to hang them over the other chair, and rolled his sleeves up muscular olive-skinned forearms as he went to the sink to wash his hands.

This wasn't happening. It couldn't be. She'd been tired after working late, she'd probably gone to sleep at the desk in her inner city office, and this was all a bad dream. Zito wasn't really here in her kitchen, opening cupboards to haul out pans, finding a jar of pasta on a shelf, demanding to know if she had red onions and tomatoes, was the garlic bulb he'd discovered with the onions all she had, and were there any cloves?

'In the cupboard next to the fridge,' she answered automatically, as she'd answered all the other questions. She watched him shake cloves into his hand and sniff at them, eyes closed, his long lashes a black crescent against golden-brown skin as he inhaled the sweet-pungent scent.

He'd always done that, checking for freshness and potency the way his grandfather had taught him.

Every time the staff who had run their big white house in Melbourne had their days off, Zito had taken Roxane down to the huge, spectacularly well-equipped kitchen and they'd make a meal together.

'Smell that,' he'd say, after doing so himself, and she'd bend over his cupped palm, breathing in the scent of newly ground pepper, an exotic spice or a freshly chopped herb before he tipped it into whatever dish he was preparing.

He'd pause in the middle of slicing an apple or a crisp, barely ripe cucumber, taste a piece and then turn and hold out another bit for her to take in her mouth.

Sometimes she'd playfully nip his fingers, inviting retribution in kind. He'd scold her for distracting him from the serious business of cooking and promise her an erotic punishment, deferred until the evening.

But not always deferred after all, so that much later they would rise from a tumbled bed and after showering together return to the kitchen, perhaps wearing only a robe apiece, and resume the interrupted preparations. The food tasted even better for the delay in one kind of gratification to the satisfaction of another.

Making a meal had been foreplay, a seductive art that Zito practised with the same unselfconscious, epicurean enjoyment that he brought to their lovemaking.

An art that had not diminished in the last year. Despite the inadequate work counter and the inconvenient placing of fridge and cooker, he demonstrated the same competence and controlled flamboyance that he had in his perfectly planned workspace with its acres of tiles and stainless steel. He even managed, apparently by instinct, to avoid hitting his head on the low-hung cupboards.

A bad dream? No, rather a blissfully sweet one, but unbearably nostalgic.

Roxane had told him once that his cooking style was like Russian ballet—so much honed masculine muscle disciplined to graceful and occasionally extravagant use within a defined space reminded her of the male dancers.

Zito laughed and said, 'Aren't they all gay?'

'Not *all* of them,' she'd protested, and he'd demanded to know how she knew, playing the jealous Latin lover, and finally swept her off to bed to prove that he was definitely, unmistakably heterosexual.

CHAPTER THREE

UNCONSCIOUSLY Roxane's lips curved in a wistful, reminiscent smile.

He'd had no need to prove his sexual orientation to her. It had been blatantly obvious from the first time she'd looked into his eyes. Despite her inexperience Roxane had recognised with a small starburst of excitement the quickly controlled but unmistakable flame of sexual desire. A flame that had ultimately consumed her, leaving behind the ashes of a marriage and a troublesome, glowing ember of reciprocal hunger.

An ember, she admitted with inward dismay, that removing herself from his dangerously flammable orbit, settling in another country, rebuilding her life without him, had failed to destroy. The sound of his voice, his breath warming her temple, the touch of his lips on the vulnerable skin of her wrist, had been enough to bring it flaring back to instant life.

'You had a bottle of Te Awa Farm Boundary in that cabinet in the other room,' Zito said, lowering a handful of spaghetti into a pot.

Roxane mentally shook herself, irrationally glad that she needn't be ashamed of her choice of that increasingly less rare commodity, a good New Zealand red. Zito had taught her to recognise decent wines. 'I'll get it.'

'No, stay there.' His hand pressed her back into the chair as he passed her on his way to the door.

But she got up all the same, needing to do something to banish the bittersweet memories. By the time Zito came back carrying an already opened bottle and two glasses, she had spread a cotton cloth on the table and set two places. And was standing staring at them, thinking, *Why am I doing this? If I had any guts I'd have shown him the door and told him not to come back.*

He poured wine into glasses, handing one to Roxane. 'Sit.'

She sat.

Habit, she told herself, watching a knife flash through an onion. During their marriage she'd become accustomed to letting him tell her what to do, and it had taken her less than sixty minutes to slip back into the mould he'd shaped for her.

Zito picked up a tomato and cut easily through the shiny red skin. *Always buy good knives.* That was something else he'd taught her. On moving into the cottage she'd treated herself to the best German stainless steel, although she could ill afford it.

Subconsciously she had still been under the spell he'd woven about her.

This mood of stunned acquiescence was due to shock. When they'd eaten she would assert herself, thank him politely and then tell him to go.

She shifted her gaze from his lean, strong fingers pinching tips of fragrant thyme from the collection of herbs on the window ledge, and reached for the luminous ruby wine, letting it slide down her throat like liquid satin.

Zito poured wine from the bottle into the concoction he was stirring on the cooker, intensifying the tantalising aroma that was making Roxane's taste buds come alive.

Soon he set before her a plate of spaghetti coils dressed with butter and herbs, topped by a mouth-watering garlic-scented sauce and garnished with fresh basil.

Then he sat opposite her, lifting his wineglass in a silent toast before picking up a fork and expertly winding spaghetti around the tines.

Instead of eating it he offered it to her, leaning across the small table, and automatically Roxane opened her lips and accepted the delicious mouthful.

Nobody cooked spaghetti sauce like Zito. Involuntarily she closed her eyes to better appreciate the taste. This too was a remembered ritual, and behind her tightly shut lids tears pricked.

She swallowed, licked a residue of sauce from her lower lip, then dared to open her eyes, hoping Zito would be concentrating on his meal.

He was smiling at her, his gaze alert and quizzical and a deliberate sexual challenge as it moved from her mouth to her eyes.

'It's…' Roxane cleared her throat. 'It's great, as always.'

He never made exactly the same sauce twice, varying the ingredients and the amounts according to his mood and what was available—or according to his assessment of *her* mood of the moment. But each variation was a masterpiece, and tonight's was no exception.

'Good.' As if he'd needed her seal of approval, he

applied himself to his plate. 'It would have been better if I'd made the spaghetti myself, but this is not bad.'

'It's made on the premises I buy it from.' He'd spoiled her for the ordinary supermarket kind.

Roxane had never mastered the tricky business of twirling spaghetti round a fork without some strands trailing all the way back to the plate, or having the whole lot perversely slide off just as she lifted it to her mouth.

Zito let his fork rest several times as he watched her efforts, a quirk of amusement on his mouth.

'Don't laugh,' she said finally, exasperated. 'You know I'm no good at this.'

He did laugh then, openly. 'Look—like this.' His hand came over hers, his fingers manipulating the fork, lifting it to her mouth with every strand neatly rolled.

She pulled her hand from his as she swallowed the proffered morsel. Dozens of times he'd tried to teach her, yet she'd failed to learn, maintaining it was in his genes, that he'd been born with a silver spaghetti fork in his mouth.

'I'm out of practice.' And with him critically studying her technique, she was clumsier than usual. 'I hardly ever eat pasta now.' What they were having was left over from a recent dinner she'd made for a couple of friends.

'No wonder you've got thinner.' His penetrating glance at her figure disapproved.

'I'm not thin!'

'Thinner, I said,' he corrected. 'You're as lovely as ever—'

'Thank you.' Her voice was brittle.

'—but you've lost weight.'

'I'm getting more exercise than I used to. It's healthy.' She'd begun walking to work to save the bus fare when she'd been living in rental accommodation and her casual job wasn't paying much. But she'd enjoyed the early morning exercise, except when Auckland's fickle weather turned nasty. Her present job being largely desk-bound, walking to the office was a good way of keeping fit. 'Do you still play squash?'

'Yes.'

At one time he'd been a state champion; trophies lined the bookcase in his study where he sometimes worked at home. But after he turned twenty-five the business had gradually absorbed more of his energies. His grandfather had retired and his father had been anxious to groom the heir to take his place in the family firm.

'How is your family?' Roxane inquired.

'Do you care?'

There it was again, that flash of acrimony like a searing flame darting through the steely armour of politeness.

'Yes, I do,' she said steadily. 'I like your parents, and I miss your sisters, they were fun and very good to me. And your grandfather is a darling.'

'But not his grandson.'

Roxane stopped trying to persuade a stubborn strand of spaghetti onto her fork and looked up. 'I told you, Zito, it wasn't—'

His closed fist thumped on the table, making the glasses jump, the wine shiver and sparkle in the light from overhead. 'You told me nothing! Nothing that made any sense!'

Roxane had jumped too, and she felt her face go taut and wary.

He said immediately, wearily, 'I didn't intend to scare you again. This can wait.'

Zito had never believed in mixing food and argument, maintaining it spoiled both of them, that each deserved to be enjoyed in its own way. Nine times out of ten, he said, after a good meal an argument didn't seem worth the effort.

Nine times out of ten he'd been right. And the tenth time, his way of resolving any issue between the two of them had been to make love to her until she could no longer think, until nothing seemed to matter but her need for him, and his for her, and every problem dissolved in the aftermath of passion. They had never, she thought with surprise, had a real quarrel.

'Eat,' he said, and she realised she'd been caught in a net of insidious remembrance while her food cooled.

A childish spurt of rebellion urged her to put down her fork and tell him she didn't want any more. Instead she twirled more spaghetti and lifted it carefully to her mouth.

'Do you feed yourself properly?' he asked her.

'I have perfectly adequate meals. Salads, lean meat, fish...soup in winter, and vegetables.'

He made a sound deep in his throat as though he didn't think much of that. 'Do you entertain?'

'My personal entertaining tends to be impromptu and informal.' The cottage couldn't comfortably be used for large gatherings. Even the dining room that previous owners had carved from the original big old-fashioned kitchen didn't have space for more than a table for six and a sideboard.

'Tell me about this job of yours,' Zito invited.

'I started work with Leon's catering firm soon after I arrived in Auckland, as casual labour. At first I was just serving food and laying tables, working lots of overtime...' She'd needed the money. 'After a couple of months he asked me to join the permanent staff.'

Leon had been impressed by her quickness, her reliability and her initiative. She remembered the inordinate thrill his praise had given her. 'I could see,' she went on, 'that some clients would have liked more than food. Someone to organise invitations, publicity, venues—take care of the details of running a successful affair.'

'*You* could see?' Zito tilted his head.

That wasn't disbelief, Roxane told herself. *It's just interest. Don't be touchy.*

'Yes,' she said firmly. 'So I ran the idea past Leon and he said, "Let's try it," and put me in charge.'

'Just like that.'

'Just like that,' she confirmed, and tried not to look smug. 'I'm very good at what I do, and now I have the salary to prove it.' Soon she would be able to afford new furniture and a few luxury items.

'Congratulations.'

'It's small beer compared to the Riccioni empire, but so far we're a roaring success.'

'Deloras isn't an empire, it's a family business,' Zito argued testily.

'A family business worth millions.' Maybe billions. She had never been privy to financial details.

'That isn't a crime. We all work very hard.'

'I know you do.' It was true of the men in the family anyway. The women weren't expected to take part directly, as had been made very clear to her.

She was to keep house, which in practice meant 'ordering' a staff of three experienced people for a household of two, preside at parties and formal dinners for which the catering was performed. by Deloras chefs and waiters, and attend functions that often seemed to have no other purpose than to allow the Deloras men to parade their success in the form of the clothes, jewels, beauty and breeding of their womenfolk.

At one of these extravaganzas, she'd complained to Zito that she felt about as useful as the magnificent carved ice centrepiece that graced the table before them. He'd smiled down at her and said, 'You're far more beautiful, and not nearly as cold.'

His eyes gleaming wickedly, he'd folded her into his arms and swung her onto the crowded area of polished floor where other couples were dancing under dimmed coloured lights to a slow, romantic tune.

Swaying rhythmically to the music, his cheek resting against her temple, he murmured to her reminders of the heat that they generated each time they came together as man and woman, his wonderfully sexy voice thickening as he described to her in explicit detail how she had reacted to him only the night before, how her responses had delighted him, how much he had enjoyed watching her total abandonment to pleasure. And what pleasure she had given him in return.

'Zito, don't!' she'd finally begged him, embarrassed by the flush that burned in her cheeks, indeed over her entire body. 'This is a public place.'

'No one can hear,' he assured her, bringing her even closer to him as he looked at her with glittering eyes. He had succeeded in arousing himself as much as he had her, she realised. His lips inches from hers, he said, 'Shall we find somewhere private?'

She was trembling. 'Here?' The function was held in the ballroom of one of Melbourne's historic houses. The whole ground floor was in use, and the upstairs region had been cordoned off.

'Outside,' Zito whispered. He leaned forward a little more, his lips barely touching hers for half a second. But instead of drawing away he bent to press another kiss to the smooth skin just behind the delicate silver and diamond pendant, one of his many exquisite gifts to her, that hung from her earlobe. The tip of his tongue traced the tiny groove, and every one of her nerve ends came alive.

Her teeth bit into her lip to stop a telltale moan escaping her throat, where her heart seemed to have lodged, a wave of sensation racing from the sensitive spot he'd teased, all the way to her toes, throbbing between her legs. For a horrifying moment she was afraid she would climax right there on the dance floor.

Pulling away, she looked at him with glazed eyes, her voice low and hoarse. 'Find somewhere.'

Without a word he turned her, a hand on her waist just below the daringly dipped back of her bronze chiffon gown. He cut a ruthless swathe through the dancers and the chattering groups gathered at the edge of the room. Someone spoke to them and Roxane tried to smile in response, her facial muscles stiff, her cheekbones heated.

Zito curtly returned the greeting but didn't slacken his stride, his arm sliding further about her waist and urging her forward.

Then he'd found a door and they were outside, where a few couples holding champagne flutes stood about on a narrow terrace lit by rows of coloured lightbulbs. It was cooler here, but not cold.

Zito didn't hesitate, plunging down a shallow flight of steps and along a brick path that narrowed as it entered a darkened thicket of shrubs and trees. Behind them Roxane heard a woman laugh, a man rumble some remark.

'Zito,' she hissed. 'People are going to guess what we're—'

'Let them.'

'Zito…' She made an effort to slow, stop.

Zito halted, both arms going about her. 'Do you care?' He kissed her quickly, thoroughly, his mouth covering hers, making her open it to him, his tongue feathering the roof of her mouth before withdrawing. His teeth gently nipped her lower lip.

'No,' she confessed recklessly, when he left her an inch between their mouths for her to reply.

Not speaking again, he propelled her further along the path, and they came on a small, unlit summerhouse. Inside Roxane saw the flutter of a light-coloured dress, heard a man's slow voice and a whispered feminine answer.

Zito gave a smothered laugh and steered Roxane off the path between a couple of white-starred shrubs, the perfumed flowers brushing her arms and leaving a subtle sweet scent on her skin. They crossed a small moonlit lawn sheltered by surrounding growth, and under the shadow of a huge old tree he paused. The night was black here, the egg-shaped half moon that hung in the sky nearly obscured by leafy branches overhead.

He kissed her again, long and deep, and his fingers found the short zipper of her dress. It was the sort of dress that didn't allow a bra, and when he slid it from her shoulders it fell about her feet.

Roxane gasped, and Zito bent, one hand still on her body, skimming down her back, and picked up the light, flimsy thing to drape it over a nearby branch.

'Are you cold?' he asked her, his hands touching her, caressing.

'No.' She was shivering, but her skin was on fire, her blood hot and heavy.

'These next,' he muttered, and her skimpy satin and lace panties joined her dress in the tree. Even through the increasing clamour of her senses, screaming for release, she was dimly grateful for his care of her clothing. Feeling silly wearing nothing but her high-heeled shoes, she slipped out of them, and a thin carpet of fallen leaves cooled her bare feet.

Somehow that added to the eroticism of this mad sexual escapade.

'You're incredibly beautiful,' Zito told her. He stood only a breath away, but not touching.

Her eyes were adjusting to the night, and she could

dimly discern the contours of his face, see the glint of his eyes. 'You can't tell,' she argued shakily. 'It's dark.'

His hands came to rest on her hips. 'There's moonlight.'

There was, filtering in moving shards through the breeze-ruffled leaves overhead. His shirt glimmered in shifting patterns of white contrasting with his dark jacket and trousers. The fact that she was naked and he was still fully dressed in formal evening clothes was suddenly a fierce turn-on. Unfair but unbelievably sexy.

'You're a nymph,' he said. 'A naiad. Something out of a fairy tale.'

But Roxane knew she was all too human, her body was telling her so, loudly. Surely he could hear the singing in her veins, the roaring tide of desire that made her temples throb, shutting out all sound but her own quickened breathing and the seduction of his voice.

Slowly he moved his hands up to her breasts, and she gave a muffled cry, placing her own hands over his to press them to her, arching her body, her head flung back.

His mouth found the taut curve of her throat, roughly exploring it, and she removed her hands from his, undoing the zipper on his trousers, freeing him with clumsy fingers.

A breath audibly dragged in his throat, and then his lips were on hers again, his tongue plunging into her mouth, and she welcomed the intimate penetration, encouraging his aggressiveness. She felt both his hands lift her, cupping her as he backed himself

against the solid trunk of the tree, and she opened
her thighs, letting him enter her smoothly, deeply,
satisfyingly, making her give a sob of pure relief.
'Love me,' she whispered, begging unashamedly.
'Oh, Zito, love me.'

CHAPTER FOUR

HE DID, thrusting even deeper, taking her over, letting her consume him in turn, holding her safe and secure while she rode the waves of pleasure, his mouth on her shoulder, her throat, her breasts, sending her higher, higher, soaring into a familiar but intensely exciting world of darkness and dizziness and delight beyond belief, beyond imagination. Where he joined her, his own gutturally expressed pleasure bringing her to yet another pulsing, uninhibited peak while he kissed her mouth again and said against the gasping little sounds that forced themselves from her lips, 'God, I love you!'

They stayed locked together for minutes, panting against each other. And then he handed her his pristine folded handkerchief and turned to retrieve her clothes, helped her dress and dropped a kiss at the top of her spine as he closed the zipper. She was still shaking, and he caught her against him and held her until she stopped, calling her darling and laughing a little anxiously but also with a hint of masculine triumph at her reaction.

They'd returned to the ballroom with her hand decorously tucked into the crook of his arm, and a glance had shown Roxane that Zito looked as well-groomed and self-possessed as always, but she headed straight for the ladies' room and a mirror.

Although her hair, which she'd worn longer then,

almost waist-length, because Zito liked it that way, had remarkably kept its casually elegant pinned-up style, her cheeks were hectically flushed, her eyes brilliant with huge glistening pupils, and her mouth moist and swollen and very red, although not a scrap of her carefully applied lipstick remained.

After repairing the damage as best she could, she'd emerged with her head high and for a decent hour or so had done her best to ignore the knowing glances and sly laughter she was sure were being directed at them, until Zito yielded to her urgent plea to take her home.

There, he'd laughed at her chagrined declaration that everyone had guessed what they'd been up to in the shrubbery, and told her it didn't matter if they had.

'I believe you're proud of it!' she accused him, and he laughed again, confirming her suspicion even as he denied the charge.

'We're married,' he said. 'We're entitled to make love where and when we choose, provided we don't frighten the horses. And it was fun, wasn't it?'

More than fun, it had been awesome, amazing, but in retrospect she was slightly horrified that they'd been unable to wait until they got home.

'I'm not going to boost your ego for you any further,' she retorted, determined to wipe the lurking smile from his mouth. But he only laughed even more before carrying her to bed and making love to her all over again, this time in a sweet, languorous fashion that nevertheless ended in a shattering climax before she slept, exhausted, in his arms.

*   *   *

'What are you thinking about?' Zito put down his fork and pushed his empty plate aside.

Jolted back to the present, Roxane raised startled eyes and immediately lowered them again, afraid that he'd read remembered passion in them. 'Nothing.' She gulped more wine before digging her own fork again into her remaining pasta. With any luck he'd think it was the wine that was making her cheeks hot. 'Do you want coffee?'

She hadn't meant to offer him coffee or anything else. But it was the first distracting thing that came into her mind.

'Not yet.' Zito emptied the bottle into her glass, picked up his own half-full one and pushed his chair backward, hooking a hand into his belt and lifting one foot to rest it on the other knee. It was a pose he'd adopted often when they were alone at home. He found it relaxing...she found it very sexy. It was so outright male and so unconsciously demonstrative of how comfortable he was with his own body.

Averting her eyes, Roxane hurriedly scooped up the remains of her meal, trying to blank her mind, pausing only to help the spaghetti down with wine.

'Shall I make it?' he asked.

'What?' Fleetingly she glanced at him.

'Shall I make the coffee?' he repeated patiently. 'You're tired.'

Thank heaven if he thought that was all it was. 'No, I'll do it.' Having offered, she could hardly retract now. Standing up, she stacked his plate on top of hers.

Zito got up too, taking them from her. 'Okay, you

do it while I deal with these.' He walked to the sink. 'You don't have a dishwasher?'

'I don't need one.' She made herself stop looking at the way his haunches moved inside the fabric of his trousers, and turned to the coffee-maker on a small trolley between the fridge and the stove. She couldn't offer Zito instant, although she knew he'd accept it courteously and drink it with every appearance of pleasure.

Or would he? As a guest he would never dream of implying any fault in the hospitality he was offered, but as her ex-husband he might feel no such obligation.

She reached for the coffee grinder and the dark roasted beans in their airtight container.

By the time the rich, heavy smell of percolating coffee hung in the air, Zito had efficiently washed up.

Roxane poured the coffee, black and unadulterated for him, sugar and a dollop of milk in hers.

Zito picked up the cups as she returned the milk to the refrigerator. 'In the front room?' he asked her.

No, she wanted to say. It was much too intimate. She'd arranged the furniture for a few people to comfortably converse.

No good excuse came to mind; the kitchen was pretty and functional but despite the thin cushions the cheap wooden chairs lacked a certain degree of comfort. She compromised with a shrug, implying the choice was his.

Taking the shrug for agreement, Zito carried the cups into the living room and placed them on the table that separated the side-by-side armchairs from the sofa.

But when she had chosen a chair he lowered himself into the other before wrapping his hand about his coffee cup and inhaling sensuously, his eyes closing—the heat of the cup, the tiny wisp of steam, the rich aroma all part of a deeply sensuous experience before he'd even tasted it. The familiar ritual renewed the ache in Roxane's heart.

Zito sipped appreciatively, then leaned back in his chair, turning his eyes toward her, and it dawned on her that she'd been awaiting his approval. Hastily she averted her own eyes and lifted her cup.

'How long have you had the place?' Zito asked.

'Six months or so.' She took another sip.

'Six months.' She sensed disapproval in his tone. 'You've been alone all that time?'

Her skin prickled. 'Mostly.'

Zito moved restlessly, and his knuckles whitened as he tightened his grip on the cup in his hand. Roxane lifted her curious gaze to his face, and saw an ominous fullness about his lower lip, perilously close to sulking, and fire in his eyes.

She suspected he thought she was deliberately being evasive. About to clarify that she had never lived with any man but himself, she paused. They were no longer married. What right did he have to explanations or excuses?

None, she told herself against a twinge of conscience, and held her tongue, forcing her expression to remain neutral and her body to relax into the chair.

Zito gulped more coffee as if it might stop him saying something explosive. Restraining himself.

The idea was so novel Roxane wanted to laugh. For once she felt as if she had the upper hand.

They weren't enemies, she reminded herself with compunction. So why did she feel this curious vindication?

'It's a small house,' Zito said abruptly.

Instinctively Roxane defended the cottage. 'Big enough for me.' She gave him a deliberately serene smile. 'And for the occasional visitor.'

That would give him something to think about.

The scowl was wiped away behind a bland answering smile, though a warning glitter lurked in the depths of his eyes. 'Do you have many…visitors?'

She would *not* let him intimidate her. 'Now and then.' Her mother had visited for a couple of weeks, and her English cousin had stayed for a few days while touring New Zealand. A work colleague had been a temporary boarder while hunting for an apartment.

But Zito wanted to know if she'd had a man—men—here overnight.

Leading him away from the subject, she asked, 'Where are you staying?'

He told her the name of his five-star hotel and she refrained from commenting, *Of course.* Then he said, 'Is that an invitation?'

'No!' She nearly choked on her coffee.

His face went taut and she added, 'I can't provide the kind of accommodation you're accustomed to.' Giving him justifications, palliatives. She pressed her lips together to shut herself up. Her cup was empty, but she went on cradling it to keep her hands occupied.

'I wouldn't complain about the accommodation,' he answered, 'if you were offering anything else.'

Roxane gave him a haughty stare, and he smiled, tempting her to throw the cup at him. Instead, she put it carefully onto the table.

A hint, but Zito seemed in no hurry to finish his coffee. 'Have I offended you?' he asked her.

As if he cared. 'Several times,' she answered.

His brows shot up. 'Darling...surely you haven't turned into a prude?'

'Maybe I always was—by your standards.'

'No.' He shook his head. 'Shy, perhaps. A little nervous at first, but that was to be expected, and I loved it. Loved your innocence and your sensuousness. You were brave and eager, and you very quickly learned to be adventurous.'

Following his lead, she had traversed uncharted pathways of sensuality with him, emboldened by his frank appreciation into sometimes taking the initiative, discovering things about his body and her own that none of the books and magazines she'd read had prepared her for, and to her astonished delight had found that by touching him in certain ways she could bring him to a kind of submission, could make him tremble in her arms.

But always it was he who finally took over, ensuring that her pleasure equalled his, that neither of them reached the pinnacle alone.

He'd been an experienced lover. Without being told, she'd known she wasn't the first woman to be the recipient of his intensely personal sexual attention.

No use wondering if he'd been as totally fascinated by other women's bodies as he was by hers, if he'd murmured the same admiring words, demonstrated the same absorption in the texture of their skin and hair, in the exact shape of their mouths, the curved arch of a foot, or the smoothness of a polished fingernail against his curled tongue.

Jealousy was a futile and demeaning emotion and Roxane refused to give way to it. She hadn't while she was married to him and she wouldn't now, when whoever he slept with should no longer concern her.

At the back of her mind she'd known all along that a man who immersed himself so thoroughly in physical activity of any kind, from sport to eating to sex—a man to whom indulging his senses was as natural as breathing—wouldn't have gone twelve months without a partner in his bed.

Only now that he was here in the flesh, so close she fancied she could feel the heat emanating from his body, accompanied by a teasing, elusive male scent, she could no longer pretend she didn't care.

Not to herself. But she needed to hide her feelings from him. 'Well,' she said, 'even adventurousness palls after a while, doesn't it?'

Maybe she'd shocked him a little, because he took a second to answer, turning to her with hard, disbelieving eyes. 'You were bored with our sex life?'

She'd touched a nerve. He'd hate to think he'd been less than successful in that area. 'I didn't say that. Anyway, it's pointless discussing it now.'

Backing away again, dodging the real issue. Despising herself, she met the angry scepticism in his eyes, and steeled herself not to react.

'You should have told me,' he said, ignoring her

denial. 'I could have arranged to spice it up. What would you have liked, darling? Toys, perhaps? A bit of bondage or S and M?'

Fierce antagonism rose at the crude suggestion and his jeering tone. 'I'm sure you'd have enjoyed that!' she flashed at him. Bondage would have nicely symbolised their relationship.

'I enjoyed what we had,' he told her. 'And don't tell me you didn't! You weren't faking what I saw in your face every time we made love, what I felt when your sweet body was convulsing against mine, when you were straining every muscle to bring me closer, deeper…harder.'

She looked away from him, staring unseeingly at the carpet while she tried to control the heat suffusing her being.

'That isn't why you left me,' he said.

'I never said it was.' Unable to bear his nearness any longer, Roxane stood up, taking a couple of steps away until she stopped before the empty fireplace, its curved grate and tiled surround surmounted by a mantelpiece holding a photograph of her parents alongside books and a Venetian glass vase.

She turned to face Zito. 'It had nothing to do with sex, you know that. You were a wonderful lover.' She was certain he knew that too. 'But it wasn't enough.'

He put his unfinished coffee down on the table and stood up. 'All I know is that giving you my heart, my life, my love wasn't enough for you. You walked away from all of it without so much as a goodbye.'

'The letter I wrote—'

He waved a hand angrily, making a derisive moue

with his mouth. '—told me nothing! Gratitude and assurances that it wasn't my fault, but you needed freedom to be a person in your own right—I'm surprised you didn't write that you were going off to "find yourself." Oh, and I forgot—' he snapped his fingers '—you signed it with your *love.*'

As if that had been the major, unforgivable sin. She hadn't known how else to end the anguished, muddled attempt at explanation. 'I'm sorry,' she said, wincing. 'But if you read it...' Surely she had conveyed *some* idea of her feelings, of the pressures and the growing panic that had forced her to take that drastic step.

'Of course I did! Twice, before I tore it up.'

Roxane's heart dropped several inches. He'd read her pathetic outpouring in mounting rage and incredulity, no doubt, and then relieved his feelings by destroying it.

'Maybe if you'd read it more carefully—'

'Would that have changed anything? You'd left me, given up on our marriage, so what difference could it make?'

None, she supposed. Only she had wanted him to understand, in some way. Futile, of course. If he hadn't understood when they were face to face, how could he have understood simply because she'd tried to put it in writing?

'You're right,' she said hopelessly. 'It doesn't matter now.'

Irritation crossed his face. 'What does matter to you, Roxane? Not your marriage vows, not your so-called love for me...'

Steadying her voice, she said evenly, 'Taking responsibility for myself.'

'By going back on your solemn promises to me? To God? You call that responsibility? What about *till death us do part?*'

He was striking at her most vulnerable inner self. Her conscience smote her often enough about reneging on her vows. 'I didn't know what I was doing back then,' she said. 'I wasn't as mature as I thought.'

'You were legally an adult,' he reminded her harshly.

'Then why didn't you treat me like one?'

His eyes glittered as his gaze passed over her in a telling, insolent inspection. 'I thought I did.' His voice descended to a deep purr. 'You had no complaints at the time.'

Roxane couldn't help a hot shiver of response to that explicit glance. Determined not to let him sidetrack her into those perilous pathways, she repeated, *'This is not about sex.'*

'Then tell me what it *is* about,' he challenged. 'What did I do to you that was so terrible?'

'Nothing!' she said. 'Not deliberately. You were just…you.'

She saw his jaw clench, his face going sallow. 'I was the man you fell in love with,' he reminded her after a moment. 'Did I change?'

'No,' she admitted. 'But you didn't want me to change either.'

Zito spread his hands in a gesture of exasperation. 'Why should I? You were my perfect woman, everything I ever dreamed of…until you left me.'

Maybe it was true. Maybe all he'd ever wanted in a woman was sweet compliance and great sex. And at first she'd been happy to give him that, devoting all her energy to being everything he asked of her, his perfect wife, pleasing him in every way possible. No wonder he'd been astonished and enraged when he discovered that she had needs and wants of her own that didn't necessarily coincide with his.

'You don't understand,' she told him. 'You never did.'

He said something explosively Italian, and turned on his heel to stride over to the window again as if he didn't trust himself to stay near her, then swung round and glared at her across the room. 'You've put a couple of thousand miles of ocean between us and cut off all communication, and you blame me for not understanding?'

He made a scornful sound and chopping gesture in the air, and Roxane had to hide a painful little smile. When he was under stress his ancestry showed. 'Maybe you're right,' he bit out. 'You were too young. Too young to know what love really is, to commit yourself to marriage, to permanence. I suppose you felt you were missing out on the things other people your age were doing.'

Roxane blazed at him, taking a couple of steps forward. 'You're making me sound like some stupid adolescent, sulking because I didn't have everything I wanted!'

'Is it so far from the truth?'

'*Yes!*'

She was shouting. With difficulty she regulated her tone, afraid that she sounded exactly like a rebellious teenager after all. 'You never gave me credit for being grown up. The only place you treated me like an equal was in bed!'

'Bed?' he repeated, a brief, wolfish grin showing his even, white teeth. 'We were a bit more imaginative than that, as I recall.'

'You know what I mean! Even now you're incapable of taking me seriously.'

'As seriously as you took our marriage?' he challenged.

'I did take it seriously! But in the end, it was too much…'

'Do you think running away was a grown-up method of dealing with your problems?'

'It was better than your way,' Roxane told him. 'Your only solution was to take me to—to make love to me.'

He'd always done that beautifully, using a lethally effective combination of tenderness and laughter and supreme male confidence to reduce her to a quivering mass of physical craving for him. And in the afterglow she would find her worries had receded into the recesses of her mind, for the time being quite unimportant, even if she'd been capable of summoning the energy and the clarity of thought to express them.

Zito noticed her hasty amendment and the smile reappeared, exacerbating her frustration. 'It seemed a pretty good solution to me,' he said. 'If that was all it took, whatever bothered you couldn't have been so terrible.'

A speculative, calculating look came into his eyes and he started strolling toward her, silent and focused and implacable, like a predator.

Reading his mind, Roxane inwardly exploded into a bewildering combination of sheer fury, outrageous desire, and atavistic fear. Her eyes widened as he neared her, and she clenched her fists, made an inarticulate sound and childishly stamped a foot, almost simultaneously stepping back and turning from him as if she could escape.

The next thing she knew she had lost her balance and her shoe. A blinding pain wrenched at her ankle. She gasped, fell, then her head seemed to explode and everything disappeared among whirling black spots that filled her vision before a total nothingness descended.

Distantly, she heard Zito's voice calling her name, and she was lifted and then laid down on something soft.

As reality returned, strong fingers gently probed into her hair, and something near her temple hurt enough to make her utter a small moan.

'Roxane!' Zito's voice again.

The dead weight of her limp, cold limbs started to alter and she sluggishly moved an arm. She guessed she was lying on the sofa. Zito picked up her cold hand and began massaging it. Gradually the dizzying black mist receded, and she opened her eyes to find him looking gaunt and almost pale, kneeling beside her. Somehow that pose was funny, unnatural for him.

He must have seen her lips move in an attempt at laughter, and he said hoarsely, 'Thank God. Stay right there while I phone an ambulance.'

'No,' she managed to say. 'Not necessary.'

'You knocked yourself unconscious,' he said, taking a mobile phone from a pocket and almost dropping it. She realised his fingers weren't steady. 'Your head hit the corner of the coffee table.'

'I was only out for a minute,' she said. 'Zito, don't!'

He had already begun dialling but she feebly grabbed his wrist and stopped him. 'Zito—it's not a real emergency.'

He frowned at her, shaking off her hand. 'You could have concussion. I won't take any risks.'

Roxane gathered her strength. '*Damn it,* Zito, just this once, will you listen to me!'

CHAPTER FIVE

His finger poised on the emergency number, Zito said impatiently, 'This is not the time to assert yourself, Roxane.'

She reached out and snatched the phone from him, struggling up. 'I've already done that, and I'm not letting you take over my life again. Leave me alone!'

The effort of sitting up made her dizzy again, and to her deep chagrin she had to sink back against the cushion he'd put behind her, and close her eyes once more.

Zito unwound her fingers from the phone. She felt his hand briefly on her forehead. 'I can't leave you alone,' he said. 'Not like this. It would be criminally negligent. Roxane...can you hear me?'

'Yes.' She opened her eyes. He looked stressed, his eyes worried and his facial muscles tight.

'You need medical attention.'

He was probably right. She ought to have her head checked after blacking out, and her ankle throbbed unpleasantly. Squinting, she saw it had swollen badly.

Zito followed her gaze and swore.

'You can call me a cab,' she compromised grudgingly, 'to take me to an emergency medical centre.'

'I'll drive you,' he said, 'if you have a car?'

Roxane shook her head, and immediately regretted

it, feeling as though someone had hit her again. 'I don't need a car, living right in the city.'

'Do you have a taxi company number?'

She gave him the number of her regular company, and after he'd dialled it he picked up her shoe from the rug. The heel was askew.

'I caught it on the step outside,' she remembered. 'It must have loosened then and I didn't notice.' Slowly this time, she sat up and pulled herself back on the cushions.

Zito dropped the shoe on the floor. 'You might as well take the other one off.' Without waiting for her consent he eased it from her stockinged foot. 'We should put a cold pack on that,' he said, frowning at the injured ankle.

'There's a packet of frozen peas in the freezer compartment of the fridge. That's supposed to be a good emergency compress.'

He nodded and went out, arriving back in minutes with the packet, and a hand towel.

She watched his bent head, trying to ignore the gentle touch of his hands as he lifted her ankle to secure the makeshift icepack with the towel. Dark hair fell over his forehead. She could see the line of his high cheekbone, the compression of his lips, the hard curve of his chin.

He looked up, catching her eyes on him, and a long moment passed before he shifted his gaze and lowered her ankle. 'Are you warm enough?' he queried roughly.

'Yes.' Surely he could see the warmth that flooded her body and scorched her cheeks? She looked away from him. 'Could you fetch a flat pair of shoes for me from my bedroom?'

'Why? You're not going to be able to walk, and I don't see you getting a shoe on that foot.'

He was right…again. Roxane moved restlessly, and a jab of pain from her ankle made her feel sick. A wave of self-pity mixed with annoyance engulfed her. Within a metaphorical five minutes of sweeping back into her life, Zito had reduced her to a state of helpless dependence.

She let fly a word that Zito had never heard from her before, and saw that she'd startled him.

'Is it that painful?' His brows drew together.

About to tell him that of course it was bloody painful but that wasn't what was driving her mad, Roxane paused when a toot from outside announced the arrival of the taxi.

'I'll open the door first,' Zito said, 'and come back for you.'

As soon as he left the room she started struggling to her feet. When he came striding back again and found her gingerly poised on one foot he said, 'What the hell are you doing?' And lifted her into his arms, so that automatically she hooked one of hers about his neck.

'Wait,' she said as they reached the hallway. 'My bag.'

Zito paused for her to collect it. 'Your key?'

He indicated it lying by the telephone, where she must have put it while she answered Leon's call. She picked it up too before he carried her out and down the steps.

He instructed the driver to wait while he closed

the house up, brushing aside Roxane's attempt to tell him there was no need to come with her, and when he'd joined her on the back seat she sat in seething silence until they arrived at the all-night clinic.

He even insisted on carrying her into the examining room, taking it for granted that he would stay. By then she was in too much pain to argue.

'Keep off the ankle for forty-eight hours,' the doctor told her after an examination and x-ray, followed by proper strapping of her foot. 'Cold packs for fifteen minutes every couple of hours, don't strap it too tightly in between, and remove the bandage at night. Rest up with the foot raised to the height of your heart. The nurse will give you an exercise sheet to strengthen the ankle when it feels better.'

He shifted his attention to her head. 'Someone needs to check on you through the night. We don't want you lapsing into unconsciousness.' He glanced at Zito. 'You can do that?'

Roxane said feebly, 'I'm sure I'm okay.'

Zito's voice overrode hers. 'Tell me what to watch for.'

'Zito,' she protested, 'you can't—'

'It's either that or you spend the night in hospital,' he said.

She knew that implacable look on his face. A hospital was probably the lesser of two evils, but she couldn't face the necessary preliminaries. She was too tired, too sore, too stressed, and didn't feel a bit well. Defeated, she admitted, 'I just want to go home to bed.'

Zito lost no time in getting her there.

Inside the cottage, he carried her up the narrow

staircase, a feat not only of strength but of dexterity, and she directed him into her room where he lowered her to the queen-size bed. He even pulled down the cover while she shifted from one side to the other.

'Can I get you a nightgown?' he asked her.

'It's under the pillow. I need the bathroom, though. You can fetch me those crutches they gave me.'

'I'll take you to the bathroom first and then get them.'

When he brought her back to the bedroom afterwards, the crutches were leaning on the night table where she could easily reach them.

Zito had poured her a glass of water, taken two of the prescribed pills out of their foil packet, and had even laid out a flimsy slip-like black satin nightgown. He probably remembered giving it to her. After leaving their home she hadn't been able to afford a whole new wardrobe and nightwear was the least important.

When she sat on the bed he said, 'I'll help you.'

His hands went to her jacket, but she shook them off. 'I'll manage,' she said sharply, 'if you just leave me.'

Zito stepped back. 'I've watched you undress hundreds of times,' he said, 'and done it for you more often than I can remember.'

'Well, you're not watching me now! Go away.' Objectively it was irrational, but she couldn't bring herself to remove her clothes in front of him. His reminder had caused a flood of erotic memories, and she took a silent, careful breath to stop herself flushing.

Zito's smile was both amused and incredulous. Then he shrugged. 'I'll be right outside.'

He gave her five minutes before tapping on the door. She was sliding under the covers when he opened it.

'Does that hurt your foot?' he asked, as she winced.

'The sheet,' she said. 'Could you just loosen it at the foot of the bed?' The duvet on top was light enough, but the sheet was constricting.

He did it for her. 'Want me to rig you a cage of some kind?'

She shook her head. 'It's fine now.'

'Good. I see you have a spare room next door. I'll be in there if you need me. In a couple of hours I'll waken you and take off that strapping for the rest of the night.'

She ought to thank him, but the words stuck in her throat. She felt weak and humiliated and furious with herself for needing his help, and with him for being the root cause. If he'd never turned up here this wouldn't have happened. 'All right,' she said grudgingly. 'There are clean sheets on the bed in there.'

After a while the throbbing in her head and ankle gradually subsided and she slipped into sleep.

Zito's hand on her shoulder roused her, his quiet voice saying her name.

She turned, her cheek brushing his hand. It was a dream, of course. As the warm pressure of his lips on her temple was a dream. Ever since she'd left him dreams had haunted her sleep, and surely this was no different.

Reluctantly she opened her eyes. It was dark, but a shaft of light from the hallway showed her Zito's broad shoulders, the shadowed outline of his face. He had lifted the covers over her foot and was gently removing the elastic bandaging, hardly hurting her at all.

'Zito.'

'You're awake,' he said, and carefully covered her bare feet again. 'Do you know where you are? Remember what happened?'

The doctor had told him to check her recall in case of concussion. 'I'm at home in my cottage. You came...I hit my head. I'm awake, it's all right.'

'Your address?'

She gave it to him.

'Good.' He replaced the blanket and kissed her forehead. 'Go back to sleep now.'

She did, muzzily comforted by the knowledge that he was there in the next room.

He roused her twice more, the second time interrupting an erotic dream that featured him in living colour. She was glad the light was too dim for him to see her face clearly.

When he left again she lapsed back into the dream world, a world where she'd never left him, and where she was as happy as she had been on their honeymoon.

They were lying on a beach in the tropical sun and there was no one else there, no sound but the faint clacking of palm trees overhead and the shush of the sea as it licked the sand. Zito touched her bare arm, smiled his dazzling smile at her, and kissed her shoulder. A delicious sensation that started at the spot where his lips lingered spread through her limbs, her entire body. She gave a murmur of delight.

Her toes, her feet, were cold, and she saw that a wave had reached them, the clear salty water cooling her skin. The little wave receded and Zito laughed and held her feet with his big hands and warmed them. He took one of her toes into his mouth, his eyes gleaming at her as she laughed back at him.

He let go her feet and drizzled warm sand onto both of them, then moved up beside her, smiled at her and kissed her mouth, his lips sure and firm. But the kiss ended too soon, and she muttered a protest and lifted her arms to bring him back to her. They felt heavy, and he captured one of her hands in his and brought it to his lips.

'Roxane?'

Her eyelids opened slowly, and she looked into Zito's dark gaze. But there was no beach, only her small room and the sunlight spying on them through the window.

Zito was sitting on the bed, holding her hand. Roxane snatched it away. Had he really kissed it or was that only in her dream? And had he kissed her mouth? She touched her tongue to her lips, but there was no way she could be sure…

'How do you feel?' he asked. 'Your feet were cold—you'd pulled the coverings off them.'

'They're warm now,' she said. 'I'm all right.'

'Not all right,' he contradicted her. 'But comfortable, I hope?'

Roxane nodded. 'I'll get up.'

She used the crutches, spurning his help, but he

followed her to the bathroom and insisted she didn't lock the door while he waited.

When she'd got back into bed he said, 'What would you like for breakfast?'

'Juice, toast, coffee. Please.'

He frowned. 'That's not a decent breakfast.'

'It's a perfectly healthy one.'

'I'll bring it up to you.'

Roxane didn't argue. The prospect of breakfast in bed was tempting, and maybe she should save her energy for a battle that really mattered.

While he was downstairs she left the bed again and hastily donned undies and a T-shirt before slipping back under the covers. Later she'd find a pair of loose pants or perhaps a skirt, that wouldn't constrict her ankle.

Zito was back in less than fifteen minutes. Besides what she'd asked for, there was also a plate of French toast and a bottle of maple syrup on the tray. 'It's for me,' he said blandly when Roxane protested.

He sat on the bed again and poured syrup onto a slice of perfect, golden-brown French toast.

She tried to ignore the delicious smell, and the sight of Zito enjoying his breakfast, but he caught her looking enviously at him.

He smiled, cut a piece and held it to her lips. 'Here.'

Roxane opened her mouth and took the morsel from him, promising herself just one bite. He cut another and she couldn't resist. They ended up sharing, as no doubt he'd intended.

As soon as he'd left with the tray she gingerly hobbled to her wardrobe, aided by the crutches.

By the time she had wriggled into a flared skirt and was back sitting on the bed, he was at the doorway again.

'Should you be getting up?' he demanded.

'I'm not going to stay in bed all day. You could pass me my hairbrush.'

He fetched it from the dressing table and handed it to her. 'You'll need something for your feet. Socks?'

Roxane consented to one sock, and he found a soft, loose one and fitted it over her damaged ankle with care, then put a slipper on the other foot.

Her eyes glazed as she looked down at his bent head. His hair was still thick and glossy, worn a little longer than he used to have it, and she remembered the surprisingly silky texture of it under her fingers.

Stifling an urge to find out if it was still the same, she gave him a muffled thanks and pulled her gaze away.

She made it on the crutches to the top of the stairs, where she paused. Behind her Zito gave a soft laugh, then he whisked the crutches away and his arms lifted her.

'You can't carry me!'

'I already did, last night.'

'Going down, though…'

'Hold tight. I promise I won't drop you.'

He made the journey step by step, and she hooked her arms about his neck and tried not to notice the dark sweep of his lashes, the lean outline of his face. He hadn't shaved this morning and there was a fuzzy shadow on his skin. Tantalisingly, she knew what it would feel like against her cheek…

He wasn't wearing his tie or jacket and the two top buttons of his shirt were open. Roxane knew the taste and texture of his skin there too, and the way intriguing little curls of chest hair tickled her palm when she stroked him.

She closed her eyes to shut out the temptation to touch, only to be assailed by other sensations—the feel of his arms holding her so securely, hard and warm yet gentle about her shoulders and under her knees, the solid wall of his chest, and the slightly salty, musky scent of him, overlaid with fresh soap. He must have washed in the downstairs washroom built into the big old laundry.

He reached the foot of the stairs and continued into the living room, placing her on the couch before he went back for the crutches.

'I've made your next icepack,' he told her. 'I'll bring it in, then strap the ankle again.'

He sat on the couch with her foot propped on his knee, the icepack wrapped in a towel as he held it to her abused ankle.

Last night's dreams floated into her consciousness, and she kept her gaze rigidly fixed on her foot.

He could hardly find any erotic thrill in the bruised, swollen flesh obscuring her ankle bone, and the bulky wrapping about the bag of crushed ice that was probably freezing his hands.

Grimacing, she said, 'It's not a pretty sight.'

'It's not ugly.' Zito glanced up. 'Just…pathetic.'

The last thing she wanted to be was pathetic. 'I hate this,' she muttered. 'Being nurse-maided by you.'

'It's necessary.' He paused, holding the pack about

her ankle with both hands. 'Do you hate it from me in particular, or being nursed in general?'

'Both.'

'Look on it as the penance for my sins,' he suggested. 'You were blaming me for all your troubles last night. And I admit to feeling some guilt for this.'

His sidelong grin invited her to laugh with him. Reluctantly, she allowed the shadow of a smile to touch her lips. 'I won't argue about that.'

He bandaged her foot again and placed a soft pillow under it on the end of the couch, kneeling to gauge the height. 'As high as your heart,' he murmured.

She couldn't help noticing that it was on a level with his heart too.

He picked up the crutches that lay on the floor, and looked at her sternly. 'If I go out for a while, will you promise not to move?'

'I'm not stupid, Zito. I'll move if I have to,' she retorted, the tilt of her chin defying him. 'You're not my keeper.'

She knew he was quite capable of taking away the crutches. Sharply, she said, 'And I'll do it with or without those!'

His lips tightened, but he stepped forward and propped the crutches against the couch.

'Thank you.'

He gave her an exasperated look. 'I hope you have the sense not to use them simply to prove your point.' He glanced at his watch. 'I'll go to my hotel and change, then bring a few things back here.'

'There's no need to come back. I'm sure you have stuff to do, people to see.'

'I don't see anyone else around to help,' he said. 'It's the weekend. I have no pressing engagements.'

'I do have friends. One of them would come if I needed someone.'

'And would you call on them?' Without waiting for an answer, he added, 'What are you so scared of, Roxane?'

'I don't know what you mean.' But she found she couldn't look at him.

After a moment he said, 'I'll be back in an hour or so. Can I bring the phone to you in case someone calls? And something to read? Or we could switch on the TV?'

'I have a mobile phone,' she said, 'in my bag. The answer service will give that number to anyone who calls. And I need to make calls of my own.'

He brought her bag and she took out a hardback notebook and pen as well as her phone. Then he fetched the newspaper from the gate for her, put her current library book within reach on the coffee table, and left with her spare key in his pocket.

Roxane skimmed the newspaper, trying to take some interest in what was happening in the world. But recent events in her own little world kept getting in the way.

She'd persuaded herself that she could live apart from Zito, made a life that was interesting and fulfilling without him. Now she could see how she'd fooled herself. No one and nothing had ever made her feel so alive, so aware of every sensation that life had to offer.

Everything seemed more colourful, more exciting, more real.

It was the way she'd felt when she first met him. *And look what that led to,* she warned herself. *Don't fall into that trap again.*

Maybe there was no trap. Zito hadn't told her he wanted her back.

The realisation brought a piercing sorrow, so that she caught her breath and had to press a hand to her midriff. The newspaper slid from her hands and spread itself on the floor.

'You fool!' she castigated herself aloud. She had no reason to feel hurt. As Zito had reminded her, she was the one who had ended their marriage, walked out on him.

She needed to think about something else. It wasn't too early to make phone calls. That was something that she didn't have to stand up for.

Zito returned carrying a flight bag and a large plastic shopping bag, and wearing casual slacks and a T-shirt. He looked terrific as always, Roxane noted with something like despair.

'I'll put these away,' he said, 'and then make some coffee? You should take more pills too. I'll bring them.'

'Thanks.' The treacherous leap of delight at the sight of him simply refused to be dismissed. She bent her head to the notebook in her lap, an excuse to hide her expression.

When he'd gone she hunched down on the couch and put the open book over her face, giving a stifled moan into the pages. This was going to be sweet torture. How long did he intend to stay?

She heard him go upstairs and the creak of the spare room floor overhead.

A welcome indignation filtered through her unwarranted euphoria. She hadn't invited him here; he'd just taken charge as he was in the habit of doing, making assumptions about her needs and brushing aside her every objection.

But the really galling thing was that she'd let him.

Time to make a stand. Literally. She struggled off the sofa, grabbed the wretched crutches and made her way to the kitchen. When Zito came down again she had coffee on and was sitting at the table with her foot propped on a chair while the percolator gurgled and spat.

Her defiant look dared him to object, and he returned it with one of such adult indulgence that she wanted to snarl, but he said nothing, denying her the chance.

She let him pour, and then he sat opposite her, still saying nothing, until she was compelled to break the silence. 'You didn't tell me how your family's been doing.'

He contemplated her for a second or two, clearly doubting her interest. 'My parents are well,' he said finally. 'My grandfather misses you.'

'I miss him, too.' She suffered a pang at the thought of the old man who had always been kind to her.

'You never even wrote to him.' His tone censured her.

She had forced herself to make a clean break, afraid that maintaining any link with his family would be an excuse to keep vicariously in contact with Zito. Besides, the old man had no secrets from his grandson. 'I was afraid he'd try to persuade me to come back.' A partial truth.

'If he had,' Zito said measuringly, 'do you think I'd have taken you back?'

Roxane's heart shrank. Her cheeks turned cold at the unexpected, deadly thrust, and it was with an effort that she was able to speak. 'The question didn't arise.' She hoped her voice sounded indifferent, but was afraid it was only reed-thin. 'Are your sisters all right?'

'Marina's new baby is a little girl—six months old now, and already bossing her brothers. Angelita has her hands full with her three. Zara's in Europe, visiting our Italian relatives.'

'And Serena?' Serena, the youngest, was closest to Roxane's own age and they'd got on well, sometimes gossiping and giggling like a couple of schoolgirls while Zito looked on with a lazy smile, his eyes filled with affection for them both.

'Serena's married.'

'To Norrie?' Serena had been seeing Norrie since her university days.

Zito nodded. 'Norrie, yes.'

'He's nice. They'll suit each other.'

'You sound quite the expert. What makes you think so?'

It was another barb, but Roxane decided to ignore it. 'They were good friends. I remember them laughing a lot together. And they're almost the same age.' She could plant a barb or two herself.

'Didn't we laugh together?' Zito asked her.

'Sometimes.' Roxane sipped her coffee. 'But more often you were laughing at me.'

He put down his cup with a clatter. 'That's not true!'

'You thought it was funny that I wasn't accustomed to having money to burn, that I couldn't bring myself to spend thousands on a dress, and when I panicked at the idea of cooking for business dinner parties.'

At the time his laughter hadn't seemed cruel, and she had been relieved when he explained that Deloras chefs would take care of the catering. But in hindsight she felt he'd been patronising. 'You even...'

'What?' he demanded as she paused there, thinking better of what she'd been going to say. 'I even...*what?*'

She looked down, then up again, holding his eyes. 'You even thought it amusing that I was a virgin. You laughed when we were ...on our honeymoon...'

His black brows drew together. 'Roxane—' his voice grated hoarsely '—that is definitely untrue. I tried to keep our lovemaking light-hearted because I knew you'd be nervous. I wanted to make your first time easy and natural, help you to relax so you wouldn't find it frightening or painful, but I was thrilled—and frankly terrified—when you told me.'

Her cup poised halfway to her mouth, she stared at him. 'Terrified?'

'I was deathly afraid of hurting you, perhaps putting you off sex altogether.'

'Well, you didn't.' The words were out before she could stop them.

Zito smiled. 'That was soon obvious. You were so

eager and yet so innocent. If I laughed then it was with relief and…joy. Utter joy—in you, in your courage and your generosity and your sweet, unforgettable passion.'

His deep voice had lowered even further. Sitting at her small, painted kitchen table in the bright light of morning, she could feel again the invisible sparks that seemed to dance over her skin, the heaviness of her limbs and the warm shivers of pleasurable anticipation that his tender preparation had created on their wedding night. She could almost imagine herself back in the sumptuous bedroom of the exclusive tropical island lodge where they'd spent twelve lazy, passion-filled days and nights.

There had been joy for her too. A joy that had lasted much longer than those twelve days. And yet…

Dismayingly, tears stung her eyes. She lifted her coffee cup to her mouth to hide them. When she replaced the cup on the table she kept her eyes cast down. 'I was a girl then. All that mattered to me was being in love.'

'What are you saying? That when you fell out of love, you were no longer interested in marriage?'

She flickered a look at him. Fell out of love? That hadn't happened. 'I'm saying there's more than sex to being married.'

'This is a new insight? Congratulations. You should share it with the world.'

Forgetting her damaged ankle, Roxane pushed her chair away from the table and half rose. 'If you're going to sneer at me—'

Her foot tangled with the chair leg and she stumbled, inadvertently putting weight on the sprained ankle. A stabbing pain forced a choked cry from her, even as Zito's chair went flying and he lunged to catch her and steady her.

'Are you hurt?' he asked urgently.

One arm was about her waist and the other hand clamped firmly just above her elbow. Her face was against his shirt, his scent filling her nostrils. Her ankle throbbed, and she gritted her teeth and thumped a closed fist against his chest. 'Damn you!' She hit him again, knowing her weak blows had no effect. 'This is all your fault!'

He held her close, and she felt him rub his cheek against her hair. 'I know, I know,' he soothed, *'carissima.'*

The endearment was another indication of his Italian heritage, although for him it was a second language, spoken, he'd laughingly told her, with an Australian accent. Not a strong one, she guessed— he'd been sent to an exclusive boys' school and taught to speak 'standard' English that to the casual listener betrayed neither his ancestry nor his birthplace. But he'd called Italian the language of love, one that he had used in their most intimate, private moments.

Roxane closed her eyes. All she wanted to do was rest against him and let him stroke her and look after her. Not to be alone any more.

Oh, no. No.

'No!' She pushed away from him, only to find that she had to rely on his support before she could reach her crutches. 'Don't!'

He arched a brow at her. 'I thought you were enjoying it.'

'I wasn't!' She adjusted the crutches and moved clumsily away from him. 'I hurt my ankle and I needed something to lean on.'

'Any time,' he murmured. '*I* enjoyed it.'

'If you want a clinging vine,' she said tartly, 'go find someone else. I'm not prepared to fill the role any more.'

'What makes you think I wanted a clinging vine?'

'You made it pretty obvious.' She swung toward the door. 'I'm going to put my foot up again.'

After a moment he said, 'I'll bring you a painkiller.'

'I don't need it, and I don't need your help.'

He didn't follow, and she heard him running the tap as she propped her foot on the end of the couch and sank against the cushions, fiercely trying to ignore the guilty knowledge that she'd been ungracious and unreasonable, even rude.

She made another business call and then picked up the library book, attempting to lose herself in the fast-moving tale of love and mystery.

It was a while before Zito reappeared, and she pretended to be absorbed in her reading.

He had bought proper cold packs and cooled them in the freezer. He fastened them inside a towel about her ankle and replaced her foot on the cushion. 'Can I get you anything else?' he asked her.

'Nothing. If you have something to do...?'

He shook his head, standing with his hands in his pockets, just a few feet from her. Even when she returned to her book she could feel him looking at her. She flicked over a page.

'Is it good?' he asked her.

'Yes.' It wasn't the author's fault that she was hardly taking in any of the story. 'I've finished with the newspaper for now, if you'd like to read it.'

He stooped and gathered it up from the floor, and although she averted her eyes Roxane was conscious of him taking a seat in one of the armchairs, apparently settling there, but she knew that he hadn't opened the newspaper.

She looked up to see him studying her, his hand loosely clasping the paper.

'You don't feel like reading?' she inquired politely.

'Never less,' he admitted. 'But don't let me disturb you.'

Roxane bit her lip. Of course he was disturbing her. It was hopeless trying to concentrate while he sat there silently.

'I have tapes and CDs,' she offered in desperation, 'if you'd like some music.'

He smiled, a faint, sardonic curving of his lips. 'And if I don't like?'

Roxane shrugged. 'Up to you.' Ostentatiously she turned back to her book.

When he got up every nerve tightened. A big hand deliberately removed the book from her grasp, and she looked up into the depths of his fathomless dark eyes.

'Stop hiding, Roxane,' he said impatiently. 'You know we have to talk.'

CHAPTER SIX

RESENTMENT stirred Roxane's blood and stiffened her muscles. 'I don't have to do anything you tell me,' she said. 'Not any more.' All the times she'd tried to talk to him, only to have him turn aside her anxieties with laughter, and still her protests with kisses...

'For God's sake!' he said. 'Will you stop treating me as if I'm some Victorian tyrant.'

'Then stop acting like one,' she snapped right back at him. 'And give me my book.'

He looked as though he would rather have hurled it across the room. Instead he dropped it into her lap.

'Is the ankle painful?' he asked abruptly.

'Not very, as long as I don't move it.'

'Then that isn't what's making you so bad-tempered.'

'*You* are making me bad-tempered,' she told him, 'just by being here.'

'I had noticed. Why?'

'I'd have thought that was obvious,' she muttered.

'As obvious as the reason you left me? Call me thick, but I still haven't figured it out. You seem to have seen me as a cross between Bluebeard and Attila the Hun.'

'I don't recall any locked room full of murdered ex-wives,' she conceded with some sarcasm. 'Although that mansion you bought was certainly big enough.'

'I have a large family,' he reminded her. 'You agreed we should have a place where we could bring everyone together without crowding.'

She hadn't argued, it was true. She'd even looked forward to it. An only child herself, she had revelled in the noisy, often drop-of-a-hat gatherings that Zito's relatives had welcomed her to.

Until his grandmother died, he'd told her, the home his grandparents had lived in for forty years had been the usual venue.

His own parents looked forward to moving into an apartment and enjoying a pleasant, relaxed retirement when the last of their children left home. His mother was ready to hand on the responsibility for entertaining family and guests, and it seemed accepted that when Zito married, it had devolved onto him—and his wife.

When Roxane demurred at the size of the house Zito had taken her to inspect before their wedding, he'd explained it would be a place for family celebrations as well as a venue for business functions. With a wicked smile he'd added that in time they would fill its numerous rooms with children of their own.

And it had been a beautiful home, spacious and welcoming and bathed in light.

'Are you still living there?' she asked him, banishing a shaft of pain at the picture in her mind of dark-eyed children that would never be.

'Why not?' He remained standing, brooding at her.

'It's useful when I'm entertaining, despite the lack of a hostess.'

She looked down at her book, playing with the corner of a page between thumb and forefinger. 'I thought...by now you might have replaced me as your...hostess.'

Somehow the silence was charged with tension, but when he spoke his voice was quiet and steady. 'My sisters sometimes help when I have business guests.' There was another pause. Without moving he said, 'They can take your place at my table. No other woman will replace my wife in my bed.'

Startled, Roxane felt the flimsy paper between her fingers tear, leaving a tiny triangle in her grasp. *Defacing a library book*, she thought guiltily. It was some kind of minor crime, wasn't it?

Her gaze went to Zito's face, the grim expression there making her quail. Her lips parted and her eyes widened with apprehension.

'You look shocked,' he said with savage irony. 'Why?'

She said the first thing she could think of. 'I'm not your wife any more.'

He moved then, violently, his hands coming out of his pockets so fast that she flinched, but although they momentarily bunched into fists, he swivelled and walked away from her, going to the window in three strides. Then he swung round again, his eyes glittering. 'You may not want to be, but we're still married, Roxane.'

'It's been a year,' she reminded him. 'You can divorce me any time. You have every right. My lawyer said the compulsory counselling requirement in

Australian law could probably be set aside, especially since I'm not living there.'

'You've discussed it with your lawyer?'

She looked away from his accusing stare. 'I didn't want you to be tied to…to a wife who'd left you. If you tell the court I refused to co-operate you'll get your divorce.'

'Thanks for your consideration,' he said caustically.

'I know you don't believe me, but I tried to make it as easy for you as I could.'

'Easy!' She guessed at the effort he put into moderating his tone before he said, 'None of it was easy for me. And I've no intention of making it easy for you. If you're desperate for a divorce, go and see your damned lawyer yourself and get him to arrange it.'

'I'm not desperate,' she said. Something in her throat was hurting. 'But if you should plan to remarry in fu—'

'Remarry?' He glared at her.

'I won't stand in your way.'

'Well, I will damn well stand in yours! I'm not tamely handing over my wife to some other man— now or ever.'

Roxane took a deep breath. 'If I wanted some other man,' she said evenly, 'it wouldn't be up to you to *hand me over!* The days are long gone when men passed women around like chattels.'

'It was a figure of speech!' He made an impatient, slashing movement with his hand.

She supposed *now or ever* was a figure of speech too. He wasn't the kind of man to live without female companionship for long. 'I assumed you'd want to be free as soon as the year was up,' she said.

'Wrong. A year, ten years, fifty if we live that long, it makes no difference—until death, Roxane—remember that?'

Roxane swallowed. Of course she remembered. And she'd meant it, but when she found she could no longer live with Zito she had known she had no right to hold him to those vows.

'You knew when you agreed to marry in my church,' he said, 'that divorce wasn't an option.'

'You haven't always stuck to the laws of your church,' she accused him. 'You weren't a virgin when you married me.'

Surely that wasn't guilt that she saw in his subtle change of expression, the tightening of his mouth, the brief shuttering of his eyes?

'I've never had any pretensions to sainthood,' he said. 'I would have been proud to come to you as you did to me, but whatever regrettable things I did in my past, I regard marriage as a sacred bond. As far as I'm concerned, we're bound together for the rest of our lives.'

A little thrill of something compounded of awe and unease ran up her spine. 'But I left you!'

'Yes,' Zito agreed grimly. 'And you covered your tracks well. Even your phone's unlisted, isn't it?'

How could he know? 'You tried to find me?' And had thought to check the New Zealand phone books?

'Of course I bloody tried! I begged and browbeat your parents, your friends—even Serena. She swore she didn't know where you were, and your parents refused to tell. I went through every avenue I could think of…and only drew the line at setting a private detective on your trail.' He paused, then admitted, 'My grandfather persuaded me that was a bad idea.'

'He did?' She ought to be grateful to the old man for that.

'After accusing me of not looking after you as I should have, and demanding to know what I'd done to drive you away. We had a blazing row.'

Roxane made a small sound of distress. 'That wasn't fair. I'm sorry, I know how close you two were.'

'I was ready to take out my anger and frustration on someone. Anyone. And he was the only person who dared to accuse me of being responsible for your desertion.'

'Oh, Zito!' She hated to think she'd caused an estrangement between them.

He looked at her with curiosity. 'We made up later,' he told her. His expression lightened fractionally, a gleam of reluctant humour in his eyes. 'He quoted that framed poster on his bedroom wall at me and tried to tell me it was an old Italian saying.'

'If you love something, let it go…?'

'That's the one. And if it's yours it will come back.' His eyes darkened to almost black. 'You didn't come back.'

'No.' It had taken some willpower, but she'd stuck it out until the first tearing agony and despair had eased, and somehow she'd survived. She had achieved what she'd set out to, made for herself an independent life.

Zito was gazing beyond her, as if looking into the past. Then he focused on her again. 'Seeing you last night was like a message from Fate. I couldn't let you disappear. I need answers, Roxane. And I intend to get them.'

For a minute or two she'd wavered, but the lack of compromise in that final declaration raised her hackles. 'What are you going to do?' she taunted him. 'Break my arm?' Looking at her bandaged ankle, she said bitterly, 'You've made a pretty good start.'

'That—' he glanced at the ankle '—was an accident that wouldn't have happened if you hadn't thrown a tantrum.'

'I did not throw a tantrum!'

'Stamping your foot at me? What would you call it?'

The humour in his voice only exacerbated her annoyance. 'I was trying to get away from you! You'd already attacked me once—'

'Attacked you?' The laughter disappeared, leaving him formidably grim. 'I stopped you from rousing the neighbourhood on a false alarm. Would you have liked having to explain to them—or the police—that you'd shrieked blue murder at the sight of your husband?'

'Ex-husband.'

Zito's teeth came together. 'Your husband.'

'Technically,' she argued. 'In name. Nothing else.'

His eyes narrowed. 'We could soon change that.'

Roxane's heart missed a beat, and plunged briefly. He looked deadly, his mouth a harsh line and the skin over his cheekbones drawn taut. She stiffened, a thread of some complex emotion making her spine tingle. 'You wouldn't...'

'Use force?' Zito asked brutally. 'You know me better than that.'

Of course she did…didn't she? Relief quickly gave way to renewed anger. For a moment she'd been physically afraid of him, overwhelmingly conscious of his size and masculine strength, and her own handicapped condition. Chagrin made her sharp. 'You were threatening me!' she accused him.

He made a scornful sound. 'I've never needed threats to get you into bed, sweetheart. Or anywhere else that we could make mad, passionate love to each other.' His eyes gleaming, he came closer to the couch, moving silently but with purpose. 'The shower,' he murmured, 'nearly every room in the house—the garden, the summerhouse. By the pool—*in* the pool. That little cove we found on our honeymoon…'

'Stay away from me!' Roxane injected as much force into her voice as she could.

He stopped less than two feet away. 'You're not afraid of me!' Renewed anger roughened his voice. Then comprehension flared in his eyes. 'You're running scared of your own feelings.' He gave a short crack of laughter. 'Because if I touch you it will be like it always was—you'll ignite like a Roman torch.'

Mortified at his accuracy, she hit back as best she could. 'You've touched me a dozen times since last night,' she said. 'And I haven't yet leapt on you and dragged you off to bed.'

'Would you like to?' he asked softly.

Despite the inward heat that his question aroused she boldly let her gaze roam over him, head to toe, deliberately objective. 'I'm not an impressionable teenager now, to be turned to a quivering jelly with a look and a touch and a few compliments and kisses.'

He returned her derisive scrutiny with one of his own, their hostile glances clashing. In a silky tone he asked, 'Is that how you felt?'

She'd fallen into that so easily. 'You made sure I did,' she told him. 'You knew how inexperienced I was. Everything's different now.'

'Everything?'

The silence was loaded. She felt her heart thumping.

When next he spoke the silk was gone, unsheathing pure, glittering steel. 'How much experience do you have now?'

'You know what I mean.' She refused to drop her gaze. 'I've grown up—finally.'

'Congratulations. And what does *that* mean, exactly?'

Goaded into a corner, she said, 'I don't need you. I don't want you.'

'You don't want me?' He looked at her with insolent calculation. Again he stepped closer, looking down at her. 'Are you sure?'

Her fingers curled. 'I told you—'

'I know,' he said irritably. 'Don't touch you. So how are you going to make it up those stairs again?'

'That's different and you know it,' Roxane snapped. 'And I wish you'd stop looming over me. I'm getting a crick in my neck.'

After a moment of edgy silence he backed away,

and dropped into the chair that he'd vacated earlier. 'Better?'

'Thank you.'

'Such good manners.'

He knew very well she was being sarcastic. She cast him a withering glance.

Her cell phone burred and, glad of the distraction, she snatched it up. 'Hello—Roxane Fabian. Oh—hi, Joanne.'

It was a friend inviting her to attend a film showing that night. Zito got up and left the room.

'I can't tonight,' she told Joanne regretfully. 'Sorry.'

'That's all right,' Joanne said, 'I'll find someone else. How are you anyway? It's a while since we got together.'

'I'm fine,' Roxanne answered, hardly hesitating. If she mentioned she'd injured herself Joanne might come round, and Zito would still be here and…

The complications were just too much. No one in New Zealand knew about her marriage. If asked, she said she was single, to save explaining.

After chatting for a while Joanne hung up with promises to keep in touch. Zito hadn't come back.

Roxane reached for her crutches, got off the sofa and hobbled through to the kitchen. Zito turned from where he'd been staring out of the window over the sink, his hands in his pockets.

'Finished your call?' he asked her. 'Can I do anything for you?'

'I'm going to the loo,' she said baldly, heading across the room to the laundry and the guest washroom.

He opened the door for her and went back to the kitchen.

After she'd washed her hands she returned to see him inspecting the contents of the refrigerator. He closed it and said, 'What would you like for lunch?'

She never kept much in the way of supplies. Zito had accustomed her to meals using only the freshest ingredients. 'Bread and cheese will do for me,' she said. 'There's sliced bread in the freezer.'

'You need vitamins,' he objected. 'I'll go and buy something. Is there anything else you want?'

'Nothing.'

'I'll see you back to your couch first.'

There was no need for that either, but she knew it was useless to say so.

He was away for less than an hour, returning with grocery bags, and an arrangement of flowers in a basket.

'You didn't have to do that,' she said.

'I wanted to. Where would you like them? They won't need water for a day or two, the florist said.'

He put them on top of her bookshelves where she could admire them, and then went off to make lunch.

He brought her fresh breads with cheeses, cold meats and raw vegetables, and tiny jars of gourmet relishes, arranged on an oval platter that he placed on the coffee table where they could both reach it.

'You enjoyed your shopping,' she remarked. He'd always haunted specialist food outlets, ever ready to try some new delicacy.

'The cheeses are New Zealand made,' he told her, pointing out the different types. He sampled each one and drew her into giving her opinion too.

When he removed the empty platter and their cups, Roxane re-studied the flowers he'd brought her, a mixture of pale pink carnations, just-unfurling deeper pink roses, and stems of old-fashioned, scented stock shading from pink to purple.

She knew he'd chosen carefully, perhaps specifying the flowers, and had the florist arrange them rather than buying the basket ready-made. Zito had always been good at that sort of thing—flowers, jewellery, all kinds of gifts. Before they were married her refusal to accept jewellery, other than his engagement ring, was one of the things that had made him laugh, in a slightly vexed way. But she loved flowers, and he'd learned that she preferred simple fragrant blooms to exotic or out-of-season ones.

She closed her eyes, breathing in the scents that teased her nostrils, bringing vividly to mind other occasions when he'd given her flowers—on her birthday, on the day he'd asked her to marry him, their wedding anniversaries, and often for no particular reason at all...

The doorbell woke her and she struggled up, automatically swinging her feet to the floor before remembering her ankle. Zito was already opening the door. Still muzzy with sleep, she heard a muffled, short conversation before the door shut and he came into the lounge. 'Ah,' he said, 'you're awake.'

He must have checked on her before. 'Do I have visitors?'

'I sent them away.'

'Without checking with me?' Her voice rose. 'Zito, you have no right—'

'Religious callers,' he cut in. 'They were anxious

to save you—or anyone. I'm sure they've only gone as far as next door, if you'd like me to call them back?' he suggested blandly.

'No, I wouldn't. How long have I been asleep?' She ran her fingers into her hair, sweeping it back behind her ears.

'About an hour. I came in to bring your pills but I didn't want to wake you. Is your head okay?'

It was woolly but she guessed that was because of her unaccustomed midday nap. 'Yes.'

'Put your foot up again. It's time for another ice-pack. Can I bring you anything else?'

'A glass of water.' Her mouth was dry. 'Please.'

He brought it for her and she took the pills he proffered and sipped the rest of the water while the ice cooled her ankle.

When he'd strapped it up again she wiggled her toes irritably.

'How's it feeling?' Zito asked, sitting in one of the chairs opposite the couch.

'All right. I'm just…'

'Bored,' he finished for her.

Not true. She was frustrated and irritable, and trying to deal with other less identifiable emotions on a deeper level. But she had never been bored when Zito was around.

Quietly, he said, 'Tell me about what you've been doing the last year.'

Roxane glanced up warily.

'I want to know how your life is. If you're happy with it.'

It wasn't an unreasonable request.

She told him about her increasingly interesting job

and her varied new circle of friends, but didn't tell
him she'd had to work on cultivating new acquain-
tances, at first forcing herself to take an interest in
other people, to be outgoing and sociable, fighting a
weak, cowardly desire to find a dark corner, curl up
in a foetal position and nurse her lacerated emotions.

She told him how she'd redecorated the cottage
after pouring her hard-earned savings into the purchase, painting and papering and sewing curtains and
cushions.

The work had kept her physically occupied, and
often tired enough to sleep when otherwise she might
have lain awake all night. But of course she didn't
mention that.

Zito fed her questions, until finally she said, 'Now
you know everything.'

'Everything?' He looked at her piercingly.

'Why don't you tell me about you?'

'Me?'

'If we're swapping stories…'

'And putting off the moment of truth?' he murmured. Not waiting for any answer, he went on,
'Business as usual. There was Serena's wedding, of
course. A couple of trips to Europe to see our suppliers and check out what's happening in the indus-
try—'

'Alone?' The word slipped out.

A glint appeared in his eyes. 'With my father, the
first time,' he said smoothly. 'He wants to give up
travelling, and I've been taking over that aspect as
well as running the financial side.'

'You must be working very hard.'

'I wanted to.' He stopped there as though he might

have said more, a grimness about his mouth. 'My parents deserve an easier life at their age.' Another pause. 'You seem to work long hours too.'

'My hours are flexible. I like it that way.'

'And you enjoy living on your own?'

It sounded like an idle remark but she knew it wasn't. 'I have only myself to please and if I don't feel like company there's no obligation to have it.' And sometimes she was lonely.

'Our house was large enough. If you'd told me you wanted your own space—'

'That's not the point.'

'Was my family too much for you?'

'No! I loved—love your family. You know that.'

'How could I know? I thought you loved me.'

It has nothing to do with not loving you. She opened her lips, then paused. Admitting it would give him an advantage that she would be wise not to concede. Zito might no longer love her, but he'd said he would never consider their marriage over.

She had the feeling that despite refraining from sending a detective after her, now he had found her he wasn't going to simply walk away.

Zito could be ruthless—she'd seen it in his business dealings and occasionally in his private life.

There was the time when Marina's husband had strayed briefly. Briefly because Zito had discovered the affair and nipped it in the bud before Marina found out. Roxane had seen the man's white, set face and hunched shoulders when he left their house after being with Zito for half an hour. 'What's wrong with him?' she had asked.

'Nothing,' Zito said tersely, 'if he has any sense.'

'He looks as if he's had a shock.'

'He needed one.' Until that day she had never seen Zito's eyes so stony hard, his mouth so grimly set. Shocked herself, she recoiled before him, very nearly frightened.

Reaching out, he touched her arm, the touch becoming a caress as his eyes softened. 'Don't worry, *carissima*. It has nothing to do with you and me. Just a family matter.'

'I am family,' she reminded him. 'And I will worry if you don't tell me what this is about.'

He hesitated, but after extracting a promise of secrecy he had told her, and then said, the grim look returning, 'I've spelled out to him just what will happen to him if he hurts my sister in any way.'

Roxane's eyes widened. 'Zito,' she gave a nervous little laugh, 'you didn't threaten to have him beaten up, did you?'

She was relieved when he laughed. 'Nothing like that.' Then, his eyes darkening, he added, 'I reminded him of what we could do to his business. I'm sure he got the point.'

Roxane hadn't known much about Marina's husband's boutique winery business. She had a vague idea that his wife's family had helped him financially, and their restaurants featured his wines on their menu, sometimes giving them special promotion. But the Deloras chain wasn't his only client. 'What could you do?' she asked.

Zito's answer was succinct and chilling, all the more so because he sounded almost casual about it. 'Break him.'

She'd had no doubt that it was no empty threat. And that he was capable of it.

I thought you loved me, Zito had just said. And he was waiting for her to say something.

Roxane moistened her lips carefully. 'I discovered that love isn't enough.'

His expression didn't change, but for once he seemed lost for words. At last he stirred, his gaze fixed on her face, and stood up. 'Then it was never love at all, was it?' he said aggressively.

He wheeled and left the room, heading toward the back of the house. Minutes later she heard cupboards opening and closing, the clashing of pans, a rattling of kitchen utensils.

He returned briefly, his face a closed mask, to ice-pack her ankle and give her a cool fruit drink, and a bit later again to ask if she didn't have any coriander seeds, but for the rest of the afternoon she was alone. She spent some more time on phone calls and finished her book.

Enticing smells began to waft from the kitchen, and Roxane made a trip to the back bathroom, more from restlessness and curiosity than an urgent need.

Zito was leaning against the counter, his head bent over a book. He hardly glanced at her, but when on her return she clumsily fetched a glass from a cupboard and turned toward the sink, he took the tumbler and poured water into it for her.

'Thank you,' she said, after drinking half. 'I could have done it, though.'

'I'll fix you a jug of water to keep by you. Do you want to finish that?'

Shaking her head in refusal, Roxane put the glass

down, fumbling for her crutch. 'You're being very kind.' It was only fair to admit it.

'For better, for worse.' His light tone didn't hide the deliberation behind the words. 'I'm not some stranger offering you mere kindness,' he said, his voice deepening. 'Even if I hadn't been partly responsible for your injury, a husband is supposed to look after his wife.'

That was his philosophy of marriage in a nutshell. 'Duty?' she asked. 'I don't think you owe me anything any more, Zito.'

'Not duty,' he said swiftly. Then, 'Honour, I suppose. I find I can't cast off my vows so easily.'

As she had. The unspoken words hung in the air between them.

'It wasn't easy for me either,' she informed him defensively. 'Not easy at all.'

'Then why the *hell* did you leave me?' Again a flash of anger broke through his control.

'I had to,' she said huskily. 'I tried to explain in my letter—I was losing myself.'

'Losing yourself.' Disgust coloured the words.

'I'm sure it sounds silly to you.'

'It sounds—'

A hiss from the cooker interrupted him, and he made a graceful dive for the overflowing saucepan, lifting it from the heat.

'I'm distracting you,' Roxane said. 'I'll leave you to it—unless I can help.'

The pungent smell of burning was strong, and he was trying to clean the mess. He threw her a look. 'You shouldn't be standing around. Get off that foot.'

She switched on the TV in the living room and

watched the news. Soon afterwards Zito came in with her dinner—loin of lamb and cooked vegetables with a tangy orange and mint sauce. He left her to eat alone.

Afterwards there was cheese and fruit. Delicious, she told him truthfully, but he brushed that aside and asked if she wanted coffee.

Roxane declined with a shake of her head. 'I need to sleep tonight. You must be tired too.' He'd stayed awake last night to check on her, and spent the day looking after her.

Zito shrugged. 'I'm fine.'

After some more pills and tending her ankle again, he sat, facing her. 'I shouldn't have insisted on talking earlier. I realise now you're not fit for it.'

Roxane looked down, rubbing an imaginary stain on the couch with her thumb. 'There's nothing wrong with my mind. We were never very good at communicating.'

'I don't recall that we had too much trouble communicating—although there were often more interesting ways than mere talk.'

'That's the problem.' Roxane looked up. 'You never would listen to me—you thought sex would solve everything.'

'Love,' Zito insisted. 'Not just sex.'

'Is there a difference, in your mind?'

'Of course there's a difference!' He scowled. 'Do you think I don't know that?'

'You used it,' she said. 'Whatever you call it, you used it to keep me in…'

Subjection was the word that came to mind, but it

sounded melodramatic and she knew that it was unjust.

'In what?' Zito demanded. 'Luxury? Oh, I see—you saw yourself as the bird in the gilded cage?'

'You don't see!' Roxane flared. 'You don't see, and you never did, because you don't want to!'

He stood up, tight-lipped and formidable. 'I didn't mean to start another argument.' His expression relaxing a little, he said in a tone of great tolerance, 'I should have known better. You can't respond rationally right now. Apparently it's quite common to have abnormal mood swings after knocking yourself out.'

CHAPTER SEVEN

Roxane tried to keep her jaw from dropping. 'M-mood swings!' *Abnormal?* 'Wherever did you get that from?'

'I bought a home medical guide when I was shopping,' Zito said. 'I've been reading all about sprains and head injuries.'

'So now you're an authority?'

He shook his head. 'Not an authority, but I've learned that even a mild concussion can have a lingering effect. Do you have a headache?'

'*No!* Well…a bit, now and then. It's nothing.'

'You're not over it yet. It's the wrong time to have a serious discussion.'

And while she was still fumbling for some kind of answer to that, he walked out of the room.

Ten minutes later he reappeared, and asked blandly if Roxane would like the TV switched on.

'No,' she said. 'You could play some music if you like.' She was still simmering, but if she blew up at him now he'd put it down to concussion. She swallowed her fury and tried to look calm…and *rational*.

While he crouched over the player she glared at his broad back. *She* was having mood swings? It was true she seemed to be on an emotional seesaw, teetering on the edge of tears one minute and wanting to throw things the next. But she didn't think it was because of the blow on her head. And Zito was equally unpredictable—most of the time soothing and patient, yet prone to moments of scorn and bitterness.

Maybe he was as unsettled by their accidental meeting as she was.

Roxane watched his careful handling of the discs as he sorted through them.

He had wonderful hands—strong and clever and amazingly capable of a delicate touch. She'd seen them meticulously arrange an artistic garnish. She'd felt them, feather-light and beautifully sensitive, exploring the most innately responsive parts of her body.

Biting her lip to counteract the images, she held her breath as Zito stood up, sliding a disc into the player before resuming his seat.

He'd chosen highlights from Broadway shows, followed by light classics, nothing too demanding or stormy. But gradually a strange depression crept over Roxane. Once they would have listened side by side, his arm about her shoulders, her head resting against him. Now they sat apart, each in their own cocoon of silence.

She moved restlessly, glanced at Zito and found him looking back at her, his eyes dark and hooded. His pose was relaxed, his legs thrust out before him, his hands loosely resting on the arms of his chair.

The track came to an end. In the short pause before another piece began something passed between her and the quiet, still man opposite. A tacit acknowledgment of the intimacy they had once shared, of the sexual chemistry that had first brought them together—a message, stark and simple. *This hasn't changed.* And for a moment she caught in his gaze a reflection of the wrenching pain within her own heart.

Roxane jerked her gaze away.

It was cruelly ironic that the next track was the love theme from a show they had seen the very first time Zito took her out. Roxane wondered if he'd noticed it named on the CD cover, or if it was just coincidence.

When the music finished Zito got up to take the disc out of the player. As he bent his head to replace it in its case Roxane said, 'I'd like to go to bed.'

He straightened quickly and turned to look at her, his eyes suddenly lit with questions.

Against her will, her breathing quickened and a warm tide raced through her. 'I'm tired,' she said. 'But I'll need your help to get up the stairs.'

'Of course,' he replied dully, and returned to his task. 'I'll take the strapping off **your ankle**.'

Maybe she imagined that he was extra tender as he unwrapped the bandage, kneeling beside the couch. 'It's looking better,' he told her. 'Not so swollen.'

'Due to your nursing.' Roxane was annoyed to hear that her voice was husky. She cleared her throat. 'I do appreciate—'

'Shh.' His fingers firmly closed her lips. 'I don't want your gratitude, Roxane.'

When he took his hand away she swallowed hard, quite unable to speak again. Her heart was hammering, and she had a crazy urge to snatch his hand back and shower kisses on it, to hold it to her cheek.

Maybe he was right about mood swings. Maybe this too was part of the aftermath of a head injury.

Or it was simply a replay of her first, vivid, incredible reaction to him. She'd persuaded herself over the past months that she'd fallen so heavily for him because she'd been young and had never before been really in love. And because Zito, ten years older and with the sophistication and assurance given by being born to money and achieving his own level of success, had dazzled her.

He still dazzled her. She had a powerful urge to drink him in with her eyes whenever he wasn't watching, and a strong desire to touch him, to have him touch her. And when he did, the way she felt was no different from the very first time he'd taken her hand in his. Dizzy and breathless and yearning.

Zito put away the icepack and came back for her. She was stiff in his arms, and he muttered, 'Relax. I know you hate this.'

Perhaps not in the way he imagined. So many times in the past he'd carried her to bed, but not to sleep.

This time he saw that she had everything she needed, made sure her crutches were within easy reach, and then left, leaving the door ajar so that he'd hear if she wanted anything during the night.

Afterwards she lay in the dark alone as always, fiercely biting into her lower lip to stop herself from calling him back.

In the morning her ankle looked less puffy, but when she cautiously tried standing up, it was obvious it wouldn't bear her weight. Sighing, she reached for the crutches.

She was halfway to the bathroom when Zito appeared, dressed in trousers and nothing else, his hair damp and tousled, and no beard shadow on his cheeks. He must have showered and shaved already.

His gaze sharpened as it passed over her red silk pyjamas to her bare feet.

'I'm all right,' she told him before he could ask. 'I'll manage on my own.'

He looked at her narrowly, then nodded and disappeared into the spare room.

When she returned his door was wide open, the bed roughly made up, but there was no sign of him.

Roxane had almost finished dressing when he tapped on her door and waited for her to call him in. An icepack in his hands, he said, 'I thought we'd start this while I make breakfast.'

'I'll come down for breakfast,' she said, sinking onto the bed to let him carry out his task.

She expected him to argue, but he said, 'All right,' in a deceptively neutral tone. 'As long as you rest the ankle.' He glanced up from adjusting the compress. 'Forty-eight hours, the doctor said.'

He'd made omelettes and bacon that he insisted on serving while she lay on the couch, and Roxanne ate without quibbling. Being waited on literally hand and foot had its advantages. Pragmatically, she advised herself to make the most of it while this lasted. Which wouldn't be much longer.

Pushing away an unwarranted shiver of apprehension, she asked, 'Did you sleep well?'

Zito gave a short, explosive laugh. 'I think the answer to that is "As well as could be expected." What about you?'

'A log,' she said, glad it was almost true. The pills

the doctor had prescribed to dull pain had probably helped.

'You seemed dead to the world all night.'

'There was no need to check on me last night!' She had a disturbing picture of him watching over her while she slept.

Zito gave her an odd, crooked smile. 'For my own peace of mind.'

Roxane had no answer to that.

He seemed mellower today. Roxane supposed she was too. Resigned to having him tend her, she was less edgy, her reactions less sharp. And perhaps he gave her less to react against. They talked, about his family and her mother's recent visit to the cottage.

'She didn't tell me she'd visited you,' he said. 'Very discreet, your parents.'

She'd made them promise not to tell him where to find her. Stunned at her decision to leave Zito, they had nevertheless loyally complied with her wishes. 'I wouldn't have told them where I was if I hadn't known I could trust them.'

Over coffee the momentary tension passed. They shared the Sunday newspaper, swapping sections. Zito read her bits from a humour column and made her laugh.

After lunch there was a classic Hitchcock movie on TV. Sitting on the end of the couch, Zito rested Roxane's foot on his thigh while he re-bandaged her ankle, glancing up now and then to watch.

He stayed there while the movie played. She was conscious of his hand resting lightly just above the bandage, and his fingers occasionally closing briefly over her toes, the pad of his thumb rubbing absently at the undersides. He'd been keeping an eye on her

toes, making sure they remained pink and warm, in-
dicating that the bandage wasn't constricting her
blood flow. Roxane told herself that was what he was
doing now.

When the credits rolled he stood up, carefully
placing her foot on a cushion. 'Can I get you anything?'

'I have everything I need.' She had water by her
now, freshened with lemon slices and cooled with
melted ice cubes.

He gave her an oddly penetrating, half-teasing
look. 'You're sure about that?'

'Yes,' she said firmly, shifting her gaze from his,
and after a moment he left her.

The day seemed to be passing quickly despite her
limited mobility. Tomorrow, presumably, Zito would
be gone. She had no obvious ill effects from her
bruised head, and her ankle was not nearly as swollen
as before. A welling of something like panic rose in
her throat.

She swung both her feet to the ground and when
Zito appeared again in the doorway with a tray of
fresh ice she was experimenting with one crutch,
hobbling across the room.

He frowned at her. 'Do you think that's sensible?'

'I have to try sometime.'

Leaning on the door jamb, he observed her critically as she made her way to the window, stopped
for a second or two, admiring the graceful droop of
the kowhai, its narrow yellow blossoms almost spent,
and the old roses and frilly pink carnations she'd
rescued from a choking overgrowth of weeds after
moving in. She'd unearthed a number of treasures

and planted new bulbs and perennials that would come up year after year.

Zito came to stand beside her. 'I didn't know you were interested in gardening.'

'I'm trying.' They had 'inherited' a gardener with the house in Melbourne, a man who had kept the grounds immaculate for years, and intimidated her with his expertise. Knowing very little herself, she had made few suggestions and never dared interfere, restraining her activities to cutting flowers for the house.

A couple of children rode skateboards dangerously fast down the sloping pavement, whooping, and she held her breath, but they negotiated the bumps and hollows with amazing skill.

Zito must have noticed her apprehension. 'They're okay,' he assured her.

'It looks awfully risky. I wonder if their parents know what they're doing.'

'Taking risks is part of growing up.'

'Yes,' she said, turning with a little difficulty. 'I know.'

He steadied her. 'That's enough. Time you put your foot up again.'

She got herself back to the couch and Zito took the crutches and propped them at the end of it. 'Your ankle could be weakened for quite a while. Liable to a repeat injury. The medical book said not to be in too much of a hurry.' He paused, looking at her, and said softly, 'Good advice, don't you think?'

'I have to work tomorrow.'

His mouth tightened, but when he spoke again his voice remained mild. 'Your boss won't expect you to turn up with a sprained ankle.'

'By tomorrow it could be perfectly normal. It's already much better.'

To her surprise he didn't argue. Instead he walked to the corner cabinet, asking, 'Do you mind if I pour myself a drink? I won't offer you one—it's too soon after your concussion.'

'Feel free.' He would anyway, and it would be petty to say otherwise, even if she wanted to refuse.

Zito poured himself vodka and helped himself to water and ice from her jug. Then he sat at the end of the couch, using his free hand to hook both her ankles up onto his knee before leaning his broad shoulders against the back of the couch.

He took a sip of his drink, then slowly turned his head and looked sombrely at her face. 'I don't feel free,' he said, 'because I'm not. And although you might wish otherwise, Roxane, neither are you.'

Roxane moistened her lips. She wished he *had* poured her a drink, but she supposed he was right—the doctor had said something about avoiding alcohol.

He tossed down the remainder of his vodka before placing the glass onto the coffee table.

When he looked at Roxane again his expression was wry and speculative. 'Maybe...' he said '...we should have had some counselling. Did you think of that before you decided to leave me?'

Surprise stopped her breath for a moment. 'If I'd suggested it,' she said, 'you'd have laughed me to scorn.' Zito had never turned to outsiders to help solve his problems. He'd have seen it as a sign of weakness, failure.

'Possibly,' he admitted after a moment. Then, with angry contempt, 'You didn't even try.'

That brought her head up and stiffened her spine. 'You just admitted you'd have thought it was a dumb idea.'

'Perhaps I wouldn't think it so dumb now,' he said slowly. 'Is that what you'd like?'

Roxane gulped. It was such a huge, unexpected concession she couldn't help being suspicious. Did he see it as a sop to her? 'I think it's probably too late for that,' she said, common sense and experience weighing in against the involuntary flutter of hope.

He tensed, his calf muscles rock hard under her legs, and she knew he was about to leap up when he remembered her feet resting across his knees. 'Is it ever too late to save a marriage? If that's what you want, that's what we'll do.'

Cautiously she said, 'You'd really go along with it?'

'Yes.' The curt monosyllable and the line between his brows told her how much he hated the prospect. 'Do I need to swear on a Bible?'

'Of course not.' Zito was a man of his word. It was how he did business, and part of the reason that, his grandfather had told her proudly, the family had doubled its fortune since he took over the financial side of its enterprise. 'But I…don't know,' she said doubtfully.

How did he think they would go about it? He couldn't stay for too long in New Zealand—he would be needed on the other side of the Tasman. This could be another attempt to bring her back to Australia.

His frown intensified. Her hesitation annoyed him, and he wasn't hiding that very well. But he clamped his lips together for a second, then said evenly,

'Think about it.' He took her ankles again in an exaggeratedly gentle hold, and stood up as he laid them back on the couch. 'Will you be all right if I go for a walk?'

'Perfectly.' He must feel cramped in this tiny house, and presumably he felt the need for exercise to work off his frustration.

When the front door closed behind him Roxane felt the sudden relaxation of muscles that she hadn't realised were so strained. She closed her eyes, trying to sort her muddled thoughts. Did he mean it? Would he really co-operate with a counsellor if they found one, or simply go through the motions to mollify her?

And was there any chance that the ingrained habits and beliefs of a lifetime, reinforced by the example of his family, perhaps bred into his genes, could be changed by a few sessions with a complete stranger?

She longed to grab at the frailest straw, against all previous experience. Her brain went round in circles, and finally stalled.

She didn't realise she'd dozed off until she woke to see Zito standing beside her.

'Oh!' She brushed a strand of hair from her eyes. 'I didn't hear you come in.'

He smiled, and her heart skipped a beat, because it was the kind of smile she remembered from what now seemed long ago, when they'd been together in their home, in their bed, and she'd turn to him as soon as she woke in the mornings, to see him propped on an elbow and watching her, waiting for her to open her eyes. Waiting to kiss her fully awake, to touch her sleep-warmed skin and bring her to singing, erotic awareness, until she parted her thighs for him in welcome and he plunged into the hot, satiny depths of her body.

Her lashes swept down, and she struggled into a sitting position. 'H-how was your walk?'

'Bracing. Are you ready for another icepack?'

'I hardly need them any more.'

'Let's have a look.'

He unwrapped the ankle and gently probed it. Roxane winced and he said, 'It's still tender, obviously. You shouldn't have tried walking on it. I'll fetch the ice.'

Afterwards he left her again and didn't come back until he carried in a dinner tray for her.

Grilled chicken, fragrant with garlic and herbs and wine. Superb, naturally. And accompanied by a chilled sparkling wine. Zito poured some into a flute for her. 'It should be safe enough by now,' he said, 'so long as you don't have too much.'

He brought in his own plate and sat across from her while they ate.

He'd even made a light, lemon-flavoured sweet that melted on her tongue and left a pleasant tang.

After he'd cleared up Zito came back into the room. Roxane tensed, expecting a demand to know if she'd thought about his astonishing suggestion of counselling.

Instead he sent her a searching look and asked if she wanted to watch TV. When she shook her head he got up and put on some more music.

Zito had switched on a side light earlier but the central light was still off. His face seemed shadowed and he wasn't looking at her, his eyelids drooping. His firm mouth had a faint downward curve, and it struck her that he looked like a man who was suffering behind a stony mask.

Had she done that to him? She'd been almost sure that he would cut her from his life and turn to someone else—perhaps a woman from a background like his own, who could be the kind of wife he wanted without feeling she was submerging her personality. The possibility had twisted her insides like a cruel knife but she had forced herself to accept it.

'I wanted you to be happy,' she murmured, the words spilling unbidden from some sad, aching place inside her.

'What?' He glanced at her.

'Nothing.' She hadn't meant him to hear.

He got up and stopped the CD player in the middle of a track. 'What did you mean?'

So he had heard, after all. 'I was thinking aloud. I didn't mean anything.'

'I didn't make *you* happy,' he said after a moment, 'did I?' He sounded as though it was difficult to get the words out. Any sort of failure was anathema to him.

'You tried,' she said, and thought that he flinched. 'Maybe too hard.'

His shoulders moved impatiently. 'How could that be?'

'I know you meant well, but I—I needed space to grow. And you wouldn't allow me any.'

It was a clumsy metaphor, and a cliché, she supposed. She fully expected him to say something cutting and shrug off her feeble attempt at analysis.

He didn't. He stood looking at her for fully half a minute, saying nothing, and then he swung into movement, prowling about the room as though he was unable to stay in one place. 'I knew I should have waited until you were older before marrying you, but I was too impatient and too...'

He stopped prowling, looking away from her, his head tilted up. 'I was afraid someone would snatch you from me.'

No chance. From the moment she'd laid eyes on him there had been no other man in the world. He was the centre of her universe. 'You did wait,' she reminded him, 'until I'd turned twenty.'

'It seemed better that you were no longer a teenager,' he acceded. 'But what difference does one day make?'

'You said I was mature.'

'You were the same age as my baby sister.'

'Serena's no baby. You told me she's a married woman now.'

A complicated look crossed his face. 'She's nearly four years older than you were when you married me.'

He turned his back abruptly, his renewed pacing taking him to the window. Outside, the street lamps cast a green glow on the parked cars and the trembling dark leaves of the trees. 'We should close the curtains,' he said.

She usually did, sensibly shutting out from prying and possibly predatory eyes the sight of a woman alone at night.

He pulled them himself, then turned to face her. 'You feel I bullied you,' he said.

'Not bullied!'

'No?'

'You simply made me feel inadequate, useless,

nothing more than a decorative touch to lighten your life and your home…'

She thought she heard the hiss of his breath being drawn in, but she couldn't clearly see his face.

'I know you didn't mean to…'

He made an impatient gesture, then jammed his hands into his pockets, with a dogged air. 'Go on. I'm listening.'

Apparently he was. 'When we were first married,' she said, 'it was nice to be looked after, pampered. Even my parents hadn't spoiled me like that. You made sure everything was done for me. The house-work, the catering, the garden—I didn't even have to cook on the staff's days off. You were so much better at it than I was.'

'We cooked together.'

'But you were in charge. You were always in charge of it all. Of everything—including me.'

He looked irritated, but waited for her to continue.

'I admit I accepted it all, enjoyed it. Even using your credit card to buy stunning clothes—'

'But you disapproved of spending too much on a dress.'

'I just couldn't get used to it, especially for a dress I'd hardly wear. But it was nice not having to worry about money if I took a fancy to something. Like a fairy tale. And you…you were every girl's storybook prince.'

He gave a harsh, scornful little laugh. 'So when,' he asked her, his eyes glittering like dark jewels, 'did the prince turn into the beast?'

CHAPTER EIGHT

'You know it wasn't like that! You were never a beast, Zito! You didn't change,' Roxane said, 'but I couldn't live in a girlish fantasy world forever.'

He looked at her across the room, animosity shimmering in the air between them. 'Our marriage was no fantasy! What are you trying to say? You came to see me as a real, flesh-and-blood male who sweated and bled, and lusted for you with my body, and you didn't like what you discovered?'

'Must you always see things in terms of the physical?' she said. 'It had nothing to do with that. It was how you viewed our relationship—how you treated me as your wife!'

'You were not mistreated!'

'I haven't accused you of that!'

'Then what—exactly—are you accusing me of?' His hands left his pockets and he threw them apart in exasperation.

Roxane took a moment to clear her thoughts, determined this time to get through to him. 'Your image of yourself was the ideal husband, the provider, the protector, giving me everything you thought I could ever need or want. I understand that, better now than I did.' Time and distance had nurtured a clearer view. 'But...' She floundered, searching for the right words.

'But you,' he said, after a second or two of intently staring at her, 'regarded me as an oppressor.'

'No!' It was difficult to articulate what she meant. 'Just a man with certain ingrained values and beliefs about women and marriage.'

'A chauvinist?' His brows rose.

'It was more subtle than that, more…complicated. You don't believe women are inferior creatures, I know that, but you had fixed ideas about how they fit into your life. Your family still operates on the old values and traditions that your grandparents brought with them from Italy.'

Zito folded his arms, his shoulder against the window frame behind him. 'I don't see much wrong with old values like loyalty and commitment.'

She didn't know if he meant it as a gibe, but it stung her. She resisted an equally stinging retort. 'I suppose "attitudes" is a better word. Especially to sex roles. You were almost as horrified as your grandfather was when I suggested getting a job.'

'I simply didn't see the need.'

He'd made that plain. And she'd seen very quickly that not only his grandfather but his parents would have regarded it as a slight on their son, a signal to outsiders that he was unable to keep his wife content.

His mother had never had a paying job in her life. She'd emigrated to Australia with her family as a girl, lived with her parents and helped in their grocery business until she married Zito's father, then devoted herself to their growing family and to entertaining her husband's friends, relatives and business contacts. Literally throwing up her hands, she had expounded volubly to Roxane on why it was unthinkable for the wife of Maurizio Riccioni to have a job outside their home.

'Wait until you have babies,' she had advised. 'They will give you plenty to do, and meantime enjoy your time with your husband. Once you have a family, believe me, you won't have too many moments to yourselves.'

But there had been no family, no babies. And she'd had all too many moments, not with Zito but on her own, when he was at the big, marble-floored offices that were the headquarters of the Deloras chain, or on a business trip somewhere meeting with wine-growers and food suppliers.

'There was no financial need,' she agreed wearily.

'I didn't forbid you to work.'

'You didn't encourage me.' And his family's opposition on his behalf had effectively deterred her. They had been so sure it would demean him, perhaps even they would respect him less for it.

'I assumed that if it was important to you, you'd do it anyway,' Zito said carelessly. He moved away from the window. 'Didn't your charity work fulfil your desire to be useful?'

She'd helped organise fundraising events for good causes. 'I suspect the charities might have benefited more if the money that went into staging concerts and balls and dressing the people attending them were to be given directly to the organisation we were trying to help,' she told him.

Glittering occasions with far too much food and drink seemed an odd way of giving to the needy. 'A few people did the actual work, the others tossed in ideas for someone else to carry out and made sure their husbands' names were on the list of benefactors.'

Zito looked slightly amused at that. 'You're not being a little unfair?'

Roxane simply shrugged without answering.

'So,' Zito said slowly, as though articulating it went against the grain, 'you felt coddled, overprotected and useless.'

It sounded feeble and petty, no reason to leave a marriage.

She tried to infuse into her words some of the remembered helplessness and frustration, a growing fear of being totally smothered, of never having the opportunity to develop into a fully adult human being. 'I felt...I felt empty and suffocated. As if I had no existence of my own.'

Zito's personality was so strong, so striking, maybe he had never realised how it overshadowed hers. She'd begun to feel no more than an extension of him, a personal accessory like his clothes or the slim gold watch, costing thousands, that he wore, he said, because of its manufacturer's reputation for reliability.

An echo of the nameless fear that had precipitated her flight curled in the pit of her stomach, and her palms were damp. 'I seemed to have no relevance to anyone—'

'No *relevance?*'

Trying to describe the emotions that had been so increasingly powerful yet difficult to name, she knew she'd floundered further and further into what must sound like irrationality. Or at best, equivocation.

'You were relevant to me,' he said.

'That's exactly it. Everything I was, everything I did, was somehow tied to my relationship with you.'

'And that's bad?' His puzzled expression gradually changed to ironic enlightenment. 'You developed a feminist consciousness?'

'You keep trying to put a label on it,' Roxane complained, her eyes flashing. 'It's too complicated for that.'

'I keep trying to understand what went wrong,' he corrected her. 'My mother said you needed a baby.'

That was when he'd announced that if she wanted a family this might be a good time.

Roxane had looked forward to having Zito's babies, but despite his light remark about filling the rooms, he'd been in no hurry, and when she'd first broached the subject early in their marriage he said she was young and they could wait.

She'd known his mother had suggested she needed occupation, and felt he was approaching the matter in the same manner as an adult might give a toy to a child to keep her out of mischief. And she'd been surprised at the depth of her resentment, the strength of her unexpected panic reaction. Although she'd hidden both from Zito.

She said, 'I don't think that would have helped.' Unless, perhaps, it had made Zito realise she was a woman, not a child herself to be humoured and indulged and never taken seriously. 'It was already too late.'

His mouth twisted. 'Tell me what would have helped,' he invited.

'If I'd been older,' she said, 'you might have

treated me differently, and maybe I could have stood up for myself more.'

'When did you need to stand up for yourself?'

'Whenever you made a decision that affected us both. Like where we were going to live—'

'I took you to see the house before signing the agreement.'

'You'd already made an offer and verbally clinched the deal.'

'With the proviso that you had to agree. If you'd hated it—'

'You knew I wouldn't hate it—'

'Well then...' He shrugged, looking both arrogant and baffled.

'—and you knew that even if I did hate it, you could talk me round. Or down. Just as you did when I wanted to redecorate the bedroom.'

'You chose the colours and fabrics.'

'After I begged you not to hire an interior designer. You insisted on having professionals to do the actual work. You didn't trust me to sew curtains or paper walls, even when I told you I'd helped my parents do it.'

'Trust had nothing to do with it!' He sounded thoroughly exasperated. 'There was no need for you to tire yourself out when we could afford to pay for the work to be done.'

'I'm young and fit, and I'd have enjoyed doing it.'

He shrugged angrily. 'If you had insisted—'

'I tried. Do you have any idea how forceful you are?'

He was looking at her fixedly. '*Did* I bully you, Roxane?'

'You just didn't consult me, even about…when to have our family. I'm glad now that we didn't—' she paused there, because a hard, almost murderous expression briefly tautened his face '—but you simply announced that you had no intention of putting me through a pregnancy and childbirth for at least a year or two.'

'I thought you were happy with that. You didn't argue. I felt you had enough adjusting to do, and at your age there was plenty of time.'

'You see?' she asked him gently. '*You* thought… You didn't ask me what I thought, about anything.'

'If you disagreed, you could have said so!'

'I didn't disagree, and it seemed futile to start an argument when I knew you were right. But I became used to going along with your every suggestion. And whenever I showed some initiative of my own you…you brushed it aside. Nothing I did was of any account.'

'I deny that!' He moved again, coming over to her, crouching at her side. He picked up one of her hands and held it, moderating his voice as he gazed down. 'Not your feelings—' he temporised reluctantly. 'I accept that's how you saw things, but I swear I never intended to belittle you in any way. If you'd told me how you felt, instead of running off—'

'I wanted to—but I was muddled then as to why I felt so…so trapped. And you never listened anyway.'

Looking away from her again, he said in a low voice, as if against his will, 'While I was walking this afternoon, I did a lot of thinking. About some of the things you said earlier.' He stopped for a moment as if he had to force out the rest. 'I guess I didn't want to hear any criticism of our marriage. I couldn't take it.'

'Why?' she asked, bewildered.

He met her eyes at last. 'I wanted to believe you were perfectly happy. Anything else would have sent me into a flat panic. Because from the time you agreed to be my wife, I was never sure I could hold you.'

'Zito!' she blurted out. 'I was *besotted* with you!'

Which was, she supposed, why she'd let him get used to ordering her life, her every move. And by the time she'd woken up to the fact that he'd taken her over completely, he'd become so accustomed to it that her feeble attempts at autonomy had not even impinged.

His hand tightened on her fingers, and his eyes blazed questions. 'You were in love,' he said. 'But I wasn't sure if it was with me or with the whole idea of love. It was all new to you. And no amount of telling myself that I was a selfish swine for talking you into marrying me could make me give you up.'

She searched his eyes. 'You must have been in love before.'

'Not that way. I knew the moment I laid eyes on you that if I let you go I'd regret it for the rest of my life. Nothing and no one would ever make up for it. Nothing and no one has, over the past hellish year, nor ever will. I tried to fool myself and everyone else that I could get over you. At first out of anger— because anger masked the hurt. Then I pretended to myself that I had loved you once, but it was finished, and the best thing I could do for both of us was to let you go.' He paused. Then starkly, his voice breaking, he added, 'I can't.'

He'd said extravagant, loving things to her before, but never had she heard such shattering emotion as in those two short words, making his voice unsteady as he held her eyes with an intensity in his gaze that shook her.

Her mouth trembled open and, shockingly unexpected, hot tears trickled down her cheeks. She had not in her wildest dreams imagined that his hurt would go so deep. Or his love survive what she had done.

Her vision blurred, and she lifted her free hand to stem the tears that wouldn't stop. But Zito's hand was already there, his thumb wiping her cheek, and then his lips were on the other cheek, kissing away the tears. He released her hand and held her face in his palms. She could feel him trembling, and her heart gave a huge leap as his breath feathered her lips.

And then he was kissing her, his mouth soft and tender, comforting, coaxing, and when hers parted beneath it, demanding and sexual.

His fingers slid behind her ears, his thumbs caressing her cheeks, smoothing strands of her hair back, even as he deepened the kiss and her head tilted further under the insistence of his mouth.

She made an inarticulate sound of capitulation and slid her arms about his neck, and he gathered her to him, pressing her back against the pillows, allowing one of his hands to sweep from her taut throat over the soft curve of her breast to her knees. He found the edge of her skirt and pushed it up, his hand skimming her inner thigh to the apex.

His touch was both frighteningly strange and achingly familiar. She shuddered and moved involuntarily against his palm, keeping him there with the pressure of her legs.

He was still kissing her, his tongue making a searching, erotic foray into her mouth, while his hand stroked her, until her whole body was consumed by shimmering sensation. Her thighs parted and she relaxed, weightless and floating on waves of building pleasure. Then he breached the flimsy barrier of cotton and she arched to him, and gave a cry, muffled by his mouth, when his encircling arm shifted and she felt his other hand on her breast.

That was when she went over the edge, when the shimmer became a starburst that consumed her, his touch the catalyst for an explosion of unimaginable power, her body totally out of control, mindless and wanton under his merciless ministration to it, as his expert stimulation wrung every last shuddering sensation from her.

He lifted his mouth, and black eyes glittered into hers, a taut smile on his lips, his cheekbones prominent while he watched the utter abandonment he'd caused, and listened to her gasping sounds of uncontrolled delight.

When at last she lay still, exhausted and panting, her eyes closed, she felt his roughened cheek against her thigh, and his lips resting there for a long second.

He pulled down her skirt, and his mouth softly touched hers, a fleeting kiss.

His arms came about her again, lifting her until

she lay against his chest. She forced her eyes open, found him looking down at her with a dark, brooding fire in his eyes.

'Bed,' he said.

Roxane nodded.

As he lifted her she closed her eyes again, listening to every breath he took, every quiet step across the room and into the hall, every careful tread up the stairway.

In the dark, he lowered her to the bed, and she made no demur when he began undressing her, taking his time.

He slipped off her shirt and undid the zip of her skirt and removed that too. He caressed her shoulders, slid down the straps of her bra, and dropped a kiss in the hollow of her throat, then gently turned her to unfasten the hook at her back. His hands stroked down her arms, taking the garment with them. Turning, she saw him straighten in the dim light from the window and quickly shuck his own clothes. Even though she could see no more than a blurred outline of wide shoulders and narrower hips, her breathing quickened.

Then he threw back the covers and lay beside her, drawing the sheet over them both.

His arm came under her and he drew her against him, holding her snugly with her back to him, his arms wrapped around her from behind.

'If you want to sleep,' he said in her ear, 'it's okay. I just need to hold you.'

Something melted inside her. She could feel his arousal, and knew he was physically unsatisfied. Yet he was prepared to postpone his own satisfaction indefinitely if she was too sated to reciprocate.

Silently she took one of his hands and moved it to her breast. She heard the quick intake of his breath, and a sigh as he let it out again. His fingers moved, tested, teased and aroused. Now both hands were stroking and sweetly tormenting. His lips brushed her nape, wandered down her spine. Sinuously, she flexed her body against him, curving her back a little so that her breasts filled his palms.

His mouth continued its slow, inexorable trail. When he reached the base of her spine his hands left her breasts and went to her hips, turning and lifting her gently as he straddled her from behind, the sheet flung back. He slipped her last garment off and then his fingers slid under her thighs, parting them slightly as he kissed the warm curves he'd exposed.

Her cheek against the pillow, Roxane gave a moan of pleasure, her hands clenching. Zito bent and kissed her just below her ear, his mouth lingering while his tongue explored.

He leaned back and moved his fingers a few inches, touched her, and she gave a small sob of anticipation and need. '*Please,*' she whispered. 'Zito…'

'I'm here,' he answered. And he was, all heat and hardness, gliding into the wet satiny folds awaiting him, filling her, moving with her, taking and being taken, thrusting and withdrawing, his fingers still weaving magic, his muscled thighs holding hers between them, and a familiar sense of wonder and mystery swept over her at the realisation that Zito was so close to her, literally inside her, something she had never learned to take for granted, every time seeming new and unique and miraculous.

Then her body took her over and she heard her own incoherent voice, knew that her hands were creasing the pillowslip, and her body was convulsing about his.

Along with the wave after wave of physical release, she was conscious of a sense of triumph as he too lost control, his fingers digging into the soft flesh of her thighs, his body tense and taut in anticipation, and then shuddering into spasms of orgiastic pleasure.

He collapsed on top of her, but after a couple of deep, gasping breaths he withdrew and rolled over, turning her and pulling her to him, her breasts against his heaving chest, and kissed her mouth, long and slow and gentle. She put a hand on his bare skin, finding it dampened with sweat, and laid her head on his shoulder.

His arm tightened. He nuzzled a kiss against her temple. 'Thank God,' he muttered. 'Are you all right, my darling? I didn't hurt your ankle?'

Roxane kissed his salty skin. 'No.' She felt floaty and unreal, but blissful. Reaching over to the bedside table, she found tissues, then settled herself against him, breathing in the tangy scent of him, and murmured, 'Mmm.'

'You still love me,' he said.

She heard an unaccustomed note of humility in his voice, tinged with wonder, and smiled against his shoulder. 'Mmm.'

Somewhere in the recesses of her mind a flashing red light was trying to penetrate the fog of delicious lethargy that obscured her thoughts, but she didn't want to take notice of it right now. It seemed sacrilege to spoil the moment. Deliberately she closed her mind's eye against the intrusive warning.

Zito's hand rested on her hip. It felt absolutely right. His body against the length of hers felt right. His chin tucked against her hair, the remembered skin textures when she let her hand stray across his chest, finding planes and shallow indentations, a fuzz of curls, and the tiny, intriguing male nipples—everything about him was so familiar it was as though his body were a part of her own.

She must have drifted off for a while. She woke when Zito eased his arm from under her.

'Zito?' She was almost convinced she was dreaming that Zito was in her bed.

'Sorry, darling,' he said. 'My arm was going to sleep, but not the rest of me.'

'You can't sleep?'

'I don't want to sleep. I'd rather lie here and listen to you sleeping.'

'Oh.' Still nicely muzzy, she smiled in the darkness. 'Did I snore?'

He laughed a little, settling against the pillows with his arms behind his head. 'No. But I can hear you breathing beside me.'

'Boring,' she said.

'Not a bit. I've been lying here and imagining all the things I want to do with you when you wake up.'

'I'm awake now.'

He turned his head. She could see the glitter of his eyes and little else. 'So come here.'

He reached for her and she went willingly into his

arms again. Later she told herself she hadn't been properly awake and wasn't responsible. But being half asleep didn't stop her from reacting with sizzling awareness to all the things Zito said he'd imagined while she was sleeping beside him. Nor from adding a few creative notions of her own. By the time they slept again, it was near dawn.

The sun streaming in the window wakened her. They hadn't drawn the curtains last night and, she realised, squinting at the small clock on the bedside table, she hadn't set her alarm either.

She was going to be late for work.

Zito lay beside her, and despite herself she couldn't help but pause to look at him, one arm flung out, his face smoothed in sleep, unaware, his bare chest rising and falling steadily above the bedclothes that had ridden down to his hips.

She eased herself from the bed, and tried to stand up, wincing as her ankle twinged emphatically.

No crutches. Neither of them had thought to bring them upstairs last night.

Last night. She glanced at Zito again, and unwelcome reality began to seep in. Last night shouldn't have happened. It was too soon. For once he had seemed ready to listen to her, had been truly trying to understand. There had been a glimmer of hope, but far too quickly it had turned to a blaze of passion, obliterating every other consideration.

They had hardly begun to scratch the surface of the real problem, and now here they were sleeping together. Sex had never been a permanent solution before. So how could it be now?

Sucking in a deep breath, she put her hand on the bedside table and tried a tentative step. She could still be stiff from sleeping. Perhaps it would get better. She left the table and took a step with her good foot. Then tried the other again.

'Aah!' She couldn't stop the strangled little shriek of pain, quickly transferring her weight to the uninjured foot.

'Roxane?' Zito stirred, then sat up, thrusting a hand into his tousled hair. 'What are you doing?'

She was stranded a few steps from the bed with nothing to hold on to. Naked, and scared to try her ankle again. 'We forgot my crutches.'

He threw back the covers and got to his feet, picked her up and deposited her on the bed, then lay beside her and pulled the covers over them both.

'You've gone white.' His hand touched her cheek, his eyes questioning.

'It hurt when I tried to stand. I'm okay now.'

'Sure?' He still looked anxious.

'Yes. Truly.'

He watched her, and in a few seconds the coldness on her cheeks and temples receded and she saw relief in Zito's eyes. 'That's better,' he said.

'You'll have to fetch the crutches for me,' she told him.

'You won't need them. I intend to keep you right here for the rest of the day.' He propped himself on one elbow, smiling his sexiest smile, and laid a possessive hand on her breast.

Terribly tempted, everything in her melting in the blaze of that smile, Roxane firmly shook her head, although already her body was responding.

He felt it, his eyes quizzical as he found a telltale hardness in his palm, and his thumb teased it into exquisite sensitivity.

'No,' Roxane said, exerting her willpower and removing his hand. 'I really do have to go to work.'

He raised his brows. 'Don't be an idiot, darling!'

Roxane kept her voice calm, although her heart began to beat faster. 'I'm supervising a big luncheon today. There's preparation to do, and I can't let Leon and our clients down. So bring me the crutches, please?'

She reached for the phone by the bed and began dialling. She was talking to Leon by the time she felt Zito slide out of the bed. 'I'll be a bit late this morning,' she was saying, 'but I'll see you in about half an hour.'

Without warning the phone was taken from her hand. Zito, tall and formidable, stood beside her, holding the receiver and looking relentlessly determined. 'No, you won't.'

CHAPTER NINE

'ZITO!' Roxane tried to grab back the receiver but he simply moved a step away.

'This is Roxane's husband,' he said pleasantly into the receiver. 'She's had an accident and isn't fit for work. You'll have to find someone else, I'm afraid.'

She made another grab, almost falling from the bed. Zito grasped her wrist and held it implacably, whether to save her or restrain her she wasn't sure.

'A sprained ankle,' he told Leon, 'and concussion. I knew you'd understand. Sure. Goodbye.'

She was shaking with rage when he put the phone back on its cradle and released her.

'You have no right to do that!' she said. He hadn't changed a bit, and the knowledge was a sickening blow to her scarcely formed hopes. 'How *dare* you!'

'Leon says he understands and he hopes you'll soon be well again.'

'I'm well now! And calling him right back.'

She reached for the phone again, but Zito bent and pulled on the cable, yanking it from the wall.

Clutching the sheet to her breasts, Roxane sat bolt upright. Quietly but with clenched teeth, she said, 'You can't do this to me, Zito.'

'I can't allow you to do this to yourself,' he said flatly. 'Be reasonable, darling!'

'That is so typical!' Her throat was raw, and a leaden ball had settled in her stomach, growing larger and heavier every second. 'You can't *allow* it? Get it into your head once and for all, Zito—*you don't own me!*'

'I never thought that—'

'Actions speak louder than words, and yours are yelling right now that you can *never* see your wife as your equal.'

'Not true. I'd do the same for any member of my family.'

'I am not a member of your family. I'm not your wife any more. If you don't file for that divorce, *I will!*'

His face seemed to lose all its colour, going grey under his natural tan. Then he said, his voice deliberate and deadly, 'After last night?'

The leaden ball dropped several inches, and nausea rose in her throat. 'It was a mistake.' Her voice wavered. 'It doesn't count.'

Zito said grittily, '*Mistake?* You don't think I'm going to return home without you after that? We belong together, Roxane. You can't turn your back on it again! I won't let you.'

'You can't *make* me come back to you, Zito. And you sure as hell can't keep me a prisoner in my own home!'

'Don't be melodramatic,' he said crushingly. 'Do you need the bathroom, or may I use it first?'

'Do what you like,' Roxane said tightly. 'You will anyway.'

He took the phone with him, increasing her impotent rage. She debated whether she could crawl downstairs while he showered, and decided she'd never make it before he emerged.

She was right. He was back within minutes, already wearing trousers, and buttoning his shirt. Tucking it into the pants, he said, 'Shall I carry you to the bathroom or bring your crutches?'

'I don't want you touching me!' Her searing glance should have withered him, but he only laughed, rather harshly.

'Don't move,' he ordered as he left the room.

As if she could. After her abortive attempt earlier she didn't even dare get herself clean undies, without at least one crutch. She had to wait for Zito to return, and then stiffly accept his offer to find fresh clothes for her.

Refusing his help to the bathroom, she had a quick, awkward shower standing on one foot, and managed to dress herself while he waited outside the door that he'd insisted she didn't lock. Tempted to do so, she curbed the immature and possibly dangerous impulse.

When she emerged he said, 'I'll bring you breakfast. Can you get back to bed on your own?'

Roxane nodded and gave him another scorching look, that he met with an infuriatingly understanding grin, and he turned to run easily down the stairs, disappearing towards the kitchen.

Once he'd gone she tightened her hold on the crutches and hobbled to the head of the stairwell, looking down. It seemed an impossibly long way.

Clumsily she seated herself on the topmost step, transferring the crutches to one hand.

With great care she eased herself to the next step, and the next.

It took a while, but eventually she arrived at the

foot of the stairs and heaved herself upright, triumphantly leaning on the crutches.

The hall telephone was only a few steps away. Roxane lifted the receiver quietly, but as she dialled, one crutch slipped and clattered to the floor.

She was giving her address to the taxi company when Zito emerged from the kitchen. Defying him with her eyes, she finished her message. 'Yes, right away, as soon as you can,' she said, and put down the receiver.

Zito said, 'How did you manage the stairs?'

'Never mind,' she answered.

'You might have had another accident.' His eyes were angry.

'I didn't. You see, Zito, I'm not as stupid and incompetent as you think.'

'I never thought that! I wouldn't have married a stupid woman.'

'Then why do you insist on treating me like one?'

'Why do you insist on acting like one?' he countered, his furious gaze sweeping over her.

'I'm acting like a responsible human being! I have a job. The prospect of losing your livelihood has never been a worry to you, but for most people getting to work on time is a priority.'

'It needn't be, for you. And if you're as indispensable as you say, your employer certainly won't sack you for taking a day or two of sick leave.'

'I told you, he needs me and I'm not going to let him down.'

'Very noble,' Zito said bitterly. 'And selective.' He didn't need to remind her that he felt she'd let him down, and their marriage, without any compunction. It was all there in his voice. Then he added, 'Just what is your relationship with your boss? He seems to have been very quick to promote you.'

Roxane started counting to ten, but barely made it past five. 'Because I was damned good at what I do! I'm not sleeping my way to the top.'

'I never suggested—'

'Then what the hell were you suggesting?'

She held his eyes, and was surprised when after a moment he closed his, tipping back his head.

'You're right,' he said. 'I apologise.'

Caught off guard, Roxane decided against answering, instead awkwardly picking up her bag from the telephone table. At least he hadn't thought to hide that. But of course he'd been sure she couldn't get down the stairs.

On cue, a discreet toot came from outside. She manoeuvred herself to the door. 'Thanks for your help this weekend,' she said stiffly, not looking at Zito. 'You can leave the key here and shut the door behind you.' Juggling crutches and bag, she laid a hand on the latch. 'Goodbye, Zito.'

He moved forward quickly, and she threw him a warning glance. 'Don't try to stop me!'

'I'm not stopping you.' She could see he was still quietly furious, but amazingly, he opened the door, then took one of the crutches and substituted his strong arm, supporting her all the way to the taxi waiting at the gate. The driver got out and opened the door and Zito helped her in, handing her the crutch.

'Thank you,' she said, bemused and a little suspicious. Why was he suddenly being so co-operative?

Perhaps because she'd persuaded him she'd make a scene if he didn't. Or that somehow she'd outwit him and go anyway. Maybe he'd begun at last to respect her determination to manage her own life.

He bent and dropped a quick kiss on her lips, hard and warm. 'Take care, and for God's sake get yourself some breakfast before you start work,' he said grittily, and shut the door.

It was too much to expect—hope?—that he would just go away after what had happened between them last night, she thought as the taxi started up the street. What a fool she was, letting her heart take over head, her body dictate to her mind, despite all she knew of Zito and of her own susceptibility.

But what sweet foolishness it had been!

Leon scolded her for turning up, though he couldn't disguise his relief. The taxi driver had helped her out of the cab and up the steps to the building, and Leon was frantically phoning round for someone to replace her for the day when she appeared.

'I'll need an assistant who can do some running around,' she admitted, 'but I can still oversee the luncheon.'

'If you're sure,' Leon said gratefully. 'But your… er…husband said—concussion?'

'I banged my head, but it's fine now.'

'I didn't know you were married.'

'I'm not, any more.' And, interpreting his complex expression, 'Zito had nothing to do with this. He just happened to be there.'

When later that afternoon Leon announced he was taking her home himself, she wasn't sure if it was out of solicitousness for her injuries or because he thought she might need protection. Either way, she was touched by his thoughtfulness.

Although he insisted on accompanying her up the steps, Roxane assured him she didn't need him to come inside.

'Well, call me if you need anything,' he said. 'Promise.'

She promised, and closed the door as he returned to the car.

Her spare key lay on the telephone table. For a few seconds she stood listening, but she'd known as soon as she opened the door that Zito wasn't there. She'd have sensed his presence. As it was, the place seemed cold and empty.

She looked at the key, and a sharp sense of loss swept over her.

All day she'd been mentally bracing herself for another confrontation, sure that Zito would follow up on the advantage he'd undoubtedly gained last night. She couldn't imagine that he'd willingly let things lie after that.

But the mute little symbol seemed to say otherwise.

She practised safely negotiating the stairs, quite successfully, made herself a light meal and ate it while watching the TV news. Then she sat through a comedy program that failed its promise to cheer her up, and made some notes about the engagement party she'd been assigned to plan. Every time a car slowed outside she held her breath, and when footsteps approached down the hill she found herself listening until they passed.

When the phone rang she almost tripped getting to it, and had to pause for a couple of deep breaths before lifting the receiver.

It was Leon, checking that she was all right.

'I'm fine,' she told him. 'But I'm glad you rang, I've some ideas I'd like to run by you.'

She had scarcely put down the receiver when the telephone shrilled again. This time she snatched it up. 'Yes?'

'Roxane,' Zito said. 'How are you coping?'

She took a second to find her voice and control it to a cool, steady tone. 'Very well. I can even manage the stairs on my own.'

'Is that safe?' His voice sharpened.

'Perfectly. I'm very careful.'

'I hope so.' There was a silence, as though he was searching for words. Or waiting for her to say something. Finally he said, 'Promise me… No.' Another hiatus, and then, 'Get in touch if you need help—at any time? Please. And don't disappear on me again. I won't harass you.'

Astonishment made her mind a blank. Was Zito actually giving up after all?'

'Roxane?'

'Th-thank you,' she said, mentally reeling. She couldn't think of another thing to add.

'Don't thank me,' he said, his voice going gritty. 'I'm flying back to Melbourne tomorrow, but you know how to contact me. Goodnight…darling.'

Then there was a click and the dial tone hummed in her ear.

Slowly she replaced the receiver and stood staring at it. Zito was leaving tomorrow.

He hadn't directly mentioned the planned duration of his visit to New Zealand, but she'd somehow gained the impression he'd be here for longer. And she had been certain he would insist on seeing her again before he left, that he'd use the potent weapon of his sexuality, as he had so emphatically, gloriously, last night, to persuade her she'd made a mistake in ending their marriage.

This was victory. Zito was leaving her to her hard-won independence, taking himself out of her life. Wasn't this what she'd kept telling him she wanted?

Why then, this overwhelming, black despair welling up from deep inside, taking her over, so that her forehead went cold and her hands clenched tightly on the crutches as she moved toward the stairs like an old, broken woman?

She spent a sleepless night relentlessly trawling through possible reasons for Zito's unprecedented withdrawal. Was he bluffing, counting on her running back to him after that one torrid night of sexual closeness? Maybe this was merely a re-enactment, more subtly carried out, of the scores of times he'd used sex to bring her to heel.

Or had he all along planned to abandon her once he'd reasserted his power to make her forget everything but her physical delight in his body, in what he could do to hers?

An act of revenge?

Then why had he insisted that their marriage wasn't over, that he would never free her from her vows?

If he'd meant it, surely he wouldn't simply shrug his shoulders now and walk away?

Unless that one night had shown him he didn't care any more. Or her defying him this morning had finally convinced him she was no longer under his domination and never would be, forcing him at last to accept defeat.

That seemed unlike everything she knew of him…

In the morning she was further than ever from any logical answer. And the ensuing weeks brought no word from Zito, no news of him, no enlightenment.

Her ankle healed and she discarded her crutches and had physiotherapy, continuing the exercises at home. In time, she assured herself, she would stop remembering Zito's vital presence in her kitchen whenever she made a lonely meal for herself, stop imagining his strong arms carrying her every time she ascended the stairs, stop longing for him beside her, holding her, every time she slipped between the sheets of her lonely bed.

She gave away the discs he'd played to the local Lions Club garage sale, rationalising that she was tired of the same old tunes. And as for the bittersweet dreams that led to her waking on a tear-stained pillow—well, they were nothing new.

Zito had dropped out of her life as abruptly as he had dropped back into it for that brief, traumatic time. Sometimes she could almost convince herself it had never happened.

Until the day she woke feeling oddly queasy, and having forced herself out of bed, glanced at the calendar on her dressing table.

She froze, mentally counting weeks and days, staring at the dates with her hands to her mouth to stifle a cry of appalled shock, a sickening dread thundering in her chest.

She waited another two weeks, trying to deny the increasing evidence. When for a couple of days she felt perfectly fine she persuaded herself that a stomach bug had caused the frequent waves of nausea, that she'd been jumping to conclusions. Her cycle had never been exactly predictable, although she didn't recall being so late before.

Then she had what appeared to be a light period. With a strange mixture of relief and sadness she dismissed the thought of pregnancy from her mind.

But a few days later while she was inspecting the food laid out in readiness for a buffet luncheon, without warning her stomach churned, violently. She made it to the ladies' room at a run, just in time to lose the meagre breakfast she'd had that morning.

Leaning over a basin, bathing her white, cold face with a trembling hand, she looked at herself in the mirror and knew that either she had some kind of sickness or…she was way more than two months pregnant.

'Not too late,' the doctor said, 'if you feel you can't have this baby. But you need to make a decision soon.'

The confirmation of a positive test brought a flood of conflicting emotions—anger, a peculiar excitement and an oddly fierce protectiveness. The amorphous possibility had become a reality that she could not ignore.

Within her she carried a new life, and whatever she did, nothing would alter the fact that it had once been there, that she and Zito had created it.

Zito. He was entitled to be told.

She went home to the cottage and spent hours walking aimlessly around it and chewing on her thumbnail while her mind revolved in inexorable circles.

She would wait another few weeks, she thought. Most miscarriages, the doctor had warned, occurred in the first trimester. If that happened Zito need never know.

Her throat tightened and hot tears scorched her eyes.

This is crazy, she thought wildly. *I don't want a baby! It's the very worst thing that could happen to me right now.*

The doctor's words came to her mind.

No. If she aborted her child she would live with regret for the rest of her life.

Had she needed any confirmation of that, it came with the terror that clutched at her the day she had persistent pains in her abdomen, and went rushing back to her doctor.

'Bed rest,' she was told, after being examined and then given an injection. 'Nature's cure. But if you do lose it, it's a signal that the foetus wasn't viable. It could be for the best.'

For the best in more ways than one, she told herself. Why didn't that bring her any comfort? Rather panic and depression. Even grief. It made no sense, but now she knew there really was a baby, her initial dismay had given way to strange new emotions, an instinct to nurture it at all costs.

She went home, took her cell phone to bed with her, and endured hours of misery and angst before she called her mother in Australia.

'You have to tell Zito,' her mother said, several days later. Despite Roxane's admittedly unconvincing protestations, Doreen Fabian had taken the first flight she could get, arriving on the cottage doorstep the morning after the phone call.

'I know.' Roxane was up now, the crisis over, though the doctor and her mother had both warned that she ought to take things easy. Doreen had been nursing before Roxane's birth, then worked part-time in a doctor's surgery near her home, and now had a full-time hospital position.

'He hasn't been in touch since…?' Doreen poured coffee and set a cup on the kitchen table in front of Roxane.

'No.' Zito's continuing silence made it all the more difficult to take the necessary step and contact him. She had no idea how he would receive the news.

'Don't you think that for the baby's sake you should try again?' Doreen asked tentatively. 'Zito was shattered when you left. He pleaded with me and your father to tell him where you were.'

'Thank you for standing firm.'

'You're our daughter. I have to admit though, sometimes I wondered if we were wrong.'

'You didn't think marrying Zito was right in the first place.'

'I wasn't sure you were ready for marriage with

anyone.' Doreen put another cup on the table for herself and sat down, stirring her coffee thoughtfully. 'But you seemed so sure, and you'd always been a sensible child, though sensitive with it. I can't help wondering if we should have pushed you out of the nest to spread your wings a bit, gain some life experience, but I thought there was plenty of time.'

Roxane supposed it hadn't occurred to her parents that she'd want to get married so soon. 'If I'd said I wanted to leave, you wouldn't have stopped me,' she said.

'No. But I was relieved you seemed happy to stay at home until you'd completed your degree.'

'I'm glad you made me do that.' Not that having a commerce degree had helped her much when she'd needed to find work after leaving Zito. She'd had no experience to back it up.

'Made you?'

'Urged,' Roxane amended. 'I should have listened to you when you said it might not be a good thing to go straight from living with my parents to living with a husband.'

Doreen gave her a sad smile. 'Zito was so obviously what used to be called a good catch, it seemed any mother's duty to encourage her daughter to marry a man like him. Maybe I should have voiced my reservations more vigorously.'

'I'd have married Zito no matter what you said.'

Doreen smiled. 'Your stubborn streak doesn't show often—I learned when you were quite small that tackling it head-on was a mistake. And mostly you were a biddable child, easily reasoned with.'

Maybe that was why Roxane had found it difficult

to stand up to Zito. Confrontation and argument had been rare in her childhood; her parents had explained rather than decreed their decisions, and even as a teenager she'd had little cause for rebellion. They trusted her judgment and she never hesitated to ask their opinion. Until she met Zito, and knew that no one's opinion would have any influence on her. She'd thought it a sign of maturity.

'Zito may not be perfect,' her mother said, 'but he's a decent man. And he loves you.'

Roxane's lips trembled, and she looked down. Maybe she'd killed that love, after all. Maybe Zito would repudiate her, and her baby.

Instinctively she put her hand over the slight swell that had begun to distend her abdomen. And felt a tiny, fairy-wing flutter under her fingers.

Startled, she raised her eyes, her breath catching. 'I think…I think it moved! Isn't it too soon?'

'It's early, but it isn't that the baby doesn't move before four months or so, it's just that it's so small most women can't feel it. With your slim figure you don't have much to mask it. You could do with a bit more weight.' Her glance held the same critical assessment as Zito's had.

'Oh.' Roxane scarcely dared breathe, staring down at her stomach as though she'd be able to see the miracle under her clothes, inside her. 'Oh, it's…I don't know. I feel so strange.' A fearful thought hit her. 'Supposing I lose it after all? I don't think I could bear it—not now.'

Her mother leaned across the table and took her free hand. 'Darling,' she said, 'phone your husband.'

*   *   *

When she told him, the line seemed dead for several seconds. Made nervous by his continued silence, Roxane blurted out, 'It needn't affect you. I can do this on my own, but you have a right to know. And my mother said I should tell you.'

'You've told your mother?'

'She's been staying with me for a while.'

'Why?' Zito demanded. 'Is something wrong?'

He was too quick. 'There was a slight problem but it's over now.'

'Put your mother on the line,' he said peremptorily.

'Zito—there's really nothing to worry about—'

'Put her on! At least she'll have the sense to tell me the truth.'

'She'll tell you just what I did.'

'Then let me speak to her!' And when she didn't answer, *'Roxane!'*

Roxane contemplated slamming down the phone. But then he said, 'For God's sake, Roxane—' and finally, as if the word were unwillingly ground out, '*—please!'*

Beneath his rising temper she sensed a desperate anxiety, whether for her or for the baby, and in the end she called her mother and handed over the receiver.

She was in the sitting room pretending to watch television when Doreen joined her, saying, 'Zito's flying over tomorrow.'

Roxane leapt to her feet, instinct urging her to flee. 'What for?'

'To see you, I suppose, and talk about your plans for the baby.'

'I have no plans.' She'd had to tell Leon the reason for her frequent hurried trips to the nearest rest room, and assured him that once the inconvenient nausea receded she'd carry on as usual. But he'd looked doubtful, and pointed out that hers was a difficult job to do with a baby in tow. A family man himself, she supposed he would know.

'Then perhaps you and Zito can make plans together,' her mother said hopefully. 'Sort something out between you.'

Like what? Roxane wondered. Maybe he'd help pay for child-care if she asked him. Her heart sank at the idea of someone else caring for her baby while she worked the long stints she had become accustomed to. But what else could she do?

Her doctor had suggested already that she cut her work hours and get as much rest as possible, adding frankly that this baby seemed not to have a firm grip and there was still a risk of losing it.

In fairness to her boss, Roxane had cast an eye over Leon's staff and singled out a promising young man, giving him more responsibility and making sure he could carry on if she wasn't there. Keeping in touch with her by phone, he'd managed very well this week.

But she couldn't give up her job. If she wasn't working she wouldn't be able to afford the mortgage, so she'd have no home for the baby. And one thing she did know about babies was that they were expensive...

Her mother said, 'I'm sure Zito will want to help out financially, at least.'

'I don't want to rely on him.' Yet it was his baby too. Really she had no choice.

She had even less after Zito arrived, kissing her mother's cheek at the door, then striding into the sitting room where Roxane sat in one of the armchairs, trying to look calm and composed.

His gaze raked her, but the loose white T-shirt she wore with blue cotton pants effectively disguised her slightly rounded abdomen.

'I'll make coffee,' Doreen said from the doorway, and left them alone before Roxane could protest.

Zito sat rather suddenly on the sofa. 'Three months, your mother said. Why didn't you tell me earlier?'

'There might not have been any point.'

His eyes narrowed, hard as obsidian. 'Meaning?'

'The doctor said it's not unusual to lose a first pregnancy.'

'Apparently you nearly did. That's why you called Doreen.'

She wished she could gauge his mood. He seemed tense and wary, and he didn't lean back against the sofa, but sat with his knees apart, his hands clasped firmly between them.

'Would you have told me,' he asked, 'if your mother hadn't pushed you into it?'

'She didn't push. I was going to anyway.'

His cocked eyebrow doubted her. 'And now that you have, what do you want me to do?'

Swallowing her pride, she said huskily, 'I thought you might like to make some…financial contribution.'

'That goes without saying. I was thinking of more basic things.'

'Nothing is more basic than money.'

He shot her an enigmatic look. 'I think we got down to something much more basic the night we conceived this child of ours.'

'So basic,' Roxane acknowledged with a flash of bitterness, 'that we didn't even think of the possible consequences.'

A strange flicker of expression altered the inflexible planes of his face. 'Didn't you?'

'Did you?' Had it crossed his mind during that wildly erotic interlude? 'Why didn't you…' He could at least have asked if she was on the pill or anything, Roxane thought angrily.

'As you kept telling me,' Zito said, 'you're responsible for yourself. I paid you the compliment of taking you at your word.'

Hoist with her own petard, and with a vengeance. She couldn't pretend she hadn't been a willing partner. And if she'd been too swept away by passion to worry about pregnancy, she could hardly throw stones at him for not stopping at the crucial moment to ask pragmatic questions.

She choked down her unreasoning anger. 'I'm still responsible for myself,' she informed him. 'And I'll take responsibility for this.'

'We both will.'

'All I need from you is some financial contribution to…to the child's upkeep.'

He looked briefly dangerous. 'If you think that I'm going to hand you money and leave you to it,' he said, 'think again. You must know this changes everything.'

Her small laugh was slightly hysterical. 'You don't need to tell me that!' Already her life was in the process of turning upside down. Hardly used yet to taking responsibility for herself, she'd been thrust into being responsible for a helpless, as yet unborn child.

'You won't be able to keep on working,' he pressed.

'I'll take maternity leave, but there's no reason I can't return to work afterwards.'

'You'd desert your baby?'

Roxane took a moment to dampen down a defensive fury. 'I wouldn't be deserting it. There are very good licensed child-care facilities—' Not for anything would she admit that she hated the thought of having to use them.

Zito made a disgusted sound. 'I'm not paying for my child to be cared for by some *facility*. You can forget that.'

Roxane felt sick. 'Are you saying if I don't do it your way, you won't help?'

She could force Zito legally to support them, she vaguely supposed, but the prospect of fighting him in court made her quail.

'I'm saying our baby has a father as well as a mother, and both of us have to think of its welfare, now. Doreen can't stay with you forever.'

Roxane felt guilty already about her mother taking emergency leave from the job she loved, and her father, with his own modest hardware business to run, would be missing his wife. 'I don't need her any more.'

'You can't be left on your own.'

'I've been on my own for over a year! I won't be the first single mother—'

'You're not a single mother! This child has a father.'

'Every child has a father…not all of them are married to the mother.'

'Are you still talking of divorce?' he demanded. 'I'm not having my child born a bastard! It was conceived within marriage and it deserves to be born in that marriage. We owe it at least that much.'

The trouble was, to Roxane it was a compelling argument. Her deepest beliefs about marriage and bringing children into the world actually meshed with his. 'It doesn't mean we have to live together.'

With deceptive quiet, he said, 'I won't leave you to fend for yourself while you carry my child. So don't even think it's going to happen.'

CHAPTER TEN

SHE might have known Zito would get his way, Roxane reflected with acid resignation, watching the tarmac of Auckland's international airport recede as their plane lifted over the Manukau Harbour a few days later.

Her mother had tried to remain neutral, but when Roxane doubled over, gasping, on the stairs to her room, bringing a white-faced Zito bounding up to scoop her into his arms and carry her to her bed, Doreen had been too obviously sick with worry.

'It looks like this is not going to be an easy pregnancy,' she told Roxane gently. 'If you insist on staying here, then so will I, at least until I'm sure you're all right.'

'Your job…'

'I'll give it up if I have to. You're more important. You and my grandchild.'

At that point Roxane had humiliated herself by bursting into tears—of chagrin, and gratitude and a myriad other emotions.

The combined pressure of her mother's good intentions and Zito's implacable logic finally forced her to give in. 'I'll stay with my parents,' she told him, willing him to accept the compromise.

'Your mother can't be with you twenty-four hours a day,' he pointed out, 'unless she leaves her job.'

'I don't need twenty-four-hour care!'

'I won't accept anything less...for the safety of our child.' He paused and then said rather grittily, 'If you really want to be with your parents I could hire a nurse for you.'

The prospect of having a stranger, however professional, watching over her in her parents' modest three-bedroom home was disconcerting, to say the least. In the end she reluctantly agreed that returning to the house she'd shared with Zito was the most practical solution. There would always be someone around to call on, and the house was big enough to accommodate a full-time nurse if necessary without making Roxane feel crowded.

The look of relief on her mother's face when Roxane said she'd think about it was the deciding factor. Needlessly disrupting her parents' lives was surely selfish. 'All right,' she'd agreed at last, tired of arguing and of trying to think of reasonable alternatives. 'Until the baby's born.'

She saw the tightening of Zito's jaw, but he merely nodded and said, 'If your doctor says it's safe, I'll arrange a flight.'

When Zito ushered her to their old room, Roxane stiffened against his light hold on her arm, balking in the doorway.

Then she saw that the king-size bed they'd shared had been replaced by two queens.

Zito shifted his hand to her waist and urged her forward. 'I thought you'd prefer your own bed,' he said quietly.

He must have arranged to have them changed in a hurry.

'I'd prefer my own room!' Roxane stepped away, facing him.

He quickly doused a flash of anger, but not before she'd seen it in his eyes. 'I don't think that's a good idea. If you need anything in the night, I'll be right here. Otherwise, I won't bother you.'

'If I need anything in the night it'll probably be the bathroom. I'll disturb your sleep.'

A faint grin replaced the anger. 'You always disturbed my sleep, one way or another. I'll sleep better here knowing you can easily wake me, than in another room. And I won't disturb *you,* I promise.'

The bedroom was big enough, boasting its own bathroom and two dressing rooms—his and hers. Even with the beds there was still room in the bay window for the two-seater sofa, and a tiny rosewood table Roxane had always liked, on which the housekeeper had arranged a posy bowl of fresh flowers.

Once they'd knocked over a vase standing there. They'd been making love on the sofa, Roxane sitting in Zito's lap as he thrust into her, his mouth on her breast, her head flung back in abandon. She was flying straight into some dazzling, dizzying light, another dimension, her legs and toes taut behind her, and was only dimly aware of her foot touching something smooth and cold.

Afterwards they'd found the flowers scattered over the carpet and water soaking into it. Mopping up with a towel, Roxane had said, 'What'll we tell Mrs. Robinson?'

'Tell her?' Zito, pausing in the act of zipping his pants, had looked blank. It wouldn't have occurred to him to explain or excuse anything to the house-keeper.

Why should it? Roxane queried herself now, dragging her gaze from the sofa and the flowers. He'd never seen the need to explain or excuse, even to his wife.

Zito had followed her gaze and now looked at her piercingly, making her colour. He couldn't read her mind, could he? Returning to the subject in haste, she said, 'I'm sure you're being unnecessarily cautious.'

'Maybe.' But he wasn't going to change his mind. 'You should probably lie down for a while after all that travelling. I'll go and give Harry a hand with your luggage.'

Harry was Mrs. Robinson's husband, the gardener and handyman Zito had kept on when they first moved into the house. Today they'd seemed glad to see her again, and fairly successful at hiding their curiosity about her return.

Left alone, she kicked off her shoes and padded to the bathroom—spotless as usual, with fresh, fluffy towels immaculately folded over the rails. Mrs. Robinson and the part-time weekly help were extremely efficient. And thoughtful. A new jar of Roxane's favourite bath oil sat on a glass shelf, and a fresh cake of matching soap nestled in the recess of the shower.

Foolish tears threatened. Her mother had told her that a tendency to cry easily went with the hormonal turbulence of pregnancy. She dashed cold water over her face and gave herself a shame-faced grimace in the mirror. 'You're a walking cliché,' she told herself. A hand on her stomach, she said sternly, 'You, my inconvenient little bundle, have a lot to answer for.'

It should have been easy to feel grateful to Zito in the ensuing weeks. His family, excited to have her back among them, came visiting separately and collectively. She was touched at their loudly expressed delight in the coming baby, and their willingness to accept her return without reservations or recriminations.

Their assumption that it was permanent caused her some unease, but to her surprise Zito said swiftly, 'That's something Roxane and I will talk about later. Right now our main concern is to make sure she gives birth safely to a healthy child.'

He took her to a gynaecologist he'd been told was Melbourne's best, and insisted she rest undisturbed every afternoon, even when her in-laws were there. But he yielded to her when she said that a visit from Serena wouldn't stop her resting.

His youngest sister came bouncing into the room, sprawled on the other bed with chin in hand and said, 'Zito's busy keeping the rest of the family at bay. Now you can tell me all about it. Just what have you and my big brother been up to?'

'You're a married woman now,' Roxane teased. 'I thought you knew all about it.'

'You know what I mean! What made you leave, and how did he make you come back?'

'I left,' Roxane said, 'because your brother was so determined that I needed looking after—and I came back for the same reason.'

Serena looked at her thoughtfully. 'Being the eldest, you know, Zito has a huge sense of responsibility.'

'I know.'

'He was always being told it was his job to look out for us girls, even when he was just a kid himself.' Serena looked down, picking at the brand-new bedspread under her fingers. 'Nonno and my dad still hold to the old patriarchal view of family, you know. They lay down the law and expect their women and children to follow it. For their own good, of course, but I'm glad Norrie isn't like that.'

'You're lucky,' Roxane said. 'You and Norrie are happy, aren't you?'

'Blissfully. Except when we're fighting.' Serena grinned at her, then sobered, her brow wrinkling in puzzlement. 'I don't remember you and Zito ever arguing. It was such a shock when you up and went like that.'

'Maybe we should have argued,' Roxane said. Brought up in a household where quarrels were avoided, she'd scarcely known how. She recalled a few spirited exchanges between Serena and her other sisters, who were really the best of friends, but Zito had seemed less volatile than most of his family, not given to explosive bouts of temper, and no more inclined than Roxane to engage in trivial arguments.

And yet, hadn't it been simply the accumulated weight of trivial incidents that had led her to destroy her marriage?

She couldn't even think of any one single moment that had triggered her decision—only a growing sense of paralysis that had overtaken her, until one day she had found herself staring into space, feeling depressed and restless and frightened, and coming to the horrifying, blinding but inevitable realisation that if she didn't get out at that very moment, she never would.

With Zito talking about babies, there was only one way out of the tender trap he'd made for her. She supposed it was the thought of imminent pregnancy that had given her the final impetus.

'So...are you arguing now?' Serena asked.

'Right now,' Roxane confessed, 'I don't even care that I never get to make a decision of my own. But I won't be pregnant forever.'

Sometimes it seemed to be taking forever. Roxane grew bigger, and the baby's movements were unmistakable now. She exercised gently and went to antenatal classes that Zito attended religiously with her. She listened to her mother's experienced advice, and did as she was told by the gynaecologist. And by Zito, who had absorbed every scrap of information and instruction and ensured that she obeyed them to the letter.

They ate at the same table, slept in the same room, and almost every day took an undemanding walk with her hand tucked into his arm.

They listened to music or watched TV, swapped books and discussed what was in the newspaper politely and without dissension. His mother took her shopping for baby clothes, mindful of Zito's admonition that Roxane mustn't get tired.

Zito was watchful and considerate and patient—and strangely aloof.

While she lived in a cocoon of pampering and preparation she was aware that Zito was keeping an emotional distance between them. Her own emotions were dangerously close to the surface these days, but it seemed that he was burying his deeper and deeper.

Her ultrasound test had disclosed that the baby was a boy. Armed with suggestions from both families, Roxane and Zito began sifting through possible names, giving them something more personal to talk about, for which Roxane at least, was grateful.

When Zito suggested it was time to furnish a nursery, a familiar wariness crept over her. 'It won't need much,' she said. 'A bassinet of course, maybe a changing table.'

'What kind of bassinet?'

'Your mother and I saw one we both liked—white cane, with primrose yellow trimmings. We could put it up in one of the spare rooms, and the changing table. I like the ones with drawers.'

'Why not in our room?'

'I thought I'd move out when the baby's born.' Roxane drew a careful breath. 'I'll be feeding it in the middle of the night.'

'Then I'll watch,' Zito said softly. His gaze lingered on the new fullness of her breasts above the curve of her pregnant figure.

Extraordinarily, she felt the centres peak and tingle, and heat swept over her. Zito was a good six feet away, relaxing in a dark red leather armchair in the downstairs sitting room, while Roxane had her feet up on the matching sofa. But if he'd stripped her and touched her she couldn't have been more aroused.

'D-don't!' she stammered involuntarily.

Zito lifted his brows.

'Don't say things like that,' Roxane said feebly. 'It's…inappropriate.'

Zito laughed. 'Inappropriate?'

'You know what I mean.'

The laughter died. He stood up, looked at her for a second, then unexpectedly came to the sofa and crouched at her side, his hand resting possessively on the swell of her stomach. 'You think it's inappropriate for me to see my son at his mother's breast?'

'You make it sound so…so…'

'Sexual?' Zito asked bluntly. 'What's so terrible about that?'

'You and I aren't—we're not that intimate any more.'

'Your choice,' he said, and his hand moved caressingly over her rounded belly, skimming upward to her breasts. 'Not mine, Roxane. Never mine.'

Then both his hands were cupping her face and turning it to him, and his mouth came down on hers, in a seeking, masterly, frankly sensual kiss.

Roxane's hands curled tightly in her lap as she resisted the urge to fling her arms about his neck and never let go. Her lips parted under the gently insistent pressure of his. Her body tautened and then relaxed, washed by a languorous, delicious warmth.

The gynaecologist had said that sex was fine as long as they took some care. Roxane hadn't told her that sex was out of the question.

Even as the thought intruded, Zito took his mouth from hers and gave her a strangely triumphant smile. 'If you change your mind,' he said, 'let me know.'

Through a haze of confused emotion, Roxane recognised danger. When all else failed, he still believed he could use her own weakness to influence her, manipulate her. Once he got her back into his bed he'd have the upper hand, be able to bend her easily to his will.

She couldn't—wouldn't let it happen all over again.

'I won't change my mind,' she said clearly. 'And I'd prefer to move into another room after the baby's born.'

For a moment their eyes clashed. She could see the surprised chagrin in his. But he said quietly, 'Whatever you want.'

'Thank you.' He'd left her with nothing more to say.

'But I'd like it if you didn't,' he added.

'You'd regret it. Being woken in the middle of the night—'

'No.'

She saw the darkening of his eyes as they rested on her, first skimming her face and then going to where she sheltered their child inside her. For a moment there was a stark hunger in his eyes that took her breath away.

'You—you never really wanted a baby,' she blurted out, astonished. He hadn't suggested it until his mother had pointed out Roxane was getting restless.

Zito returned his gaze to her face. 'I wanted this one. Desperately. Why else would I have decided to—'

His abrupt stop there left her hanging for a second

or two before enlightenment dawned in an explosive burst.

'What do you mean?' she asked, fearful of the answer.

But he didn't give her one, instead turning his shoulder to her as if about to leave the room. Increasingly sure she was right, and filled with horrified fury, Roxane said more loudly, imperiously, '*What do you mean,* Zito?'

He looked away from her almost guiltily, glancing randomly across the room at the window. 'I figured,' he said remotely, 'it was a thousand-to-one chance. A chance I was willing to take.'

Roxane gaped at him. Her heart began to thud, suffocatingly. She thought her head might explode, there was a peculiar thrumming at her temples. 'That you *decided* to take!' she repeated. 'You didn't ask me if *I* was willing!'

Blood roared in her ears until she could scarcely hear her own voice. 'Because that's what you wanted? You *wanted* to get me pregnant!' It hadn't been a passing thought, overruled by the heat of the moment, but a deliberate action.

He brought his gaze back to her. 'I hoped,' he said. 'All I had was hope.'

'For *what?* That I'd have to come running back to you?' That it would send her to him for help, perhaps make her want to stay because he could make life so much easier for her and her child. He'd planned it all. She moistened her lips, choked out the words. 'You deliberately trapped me!'

CHAPTER ELEVEN

ROXANE'S breathing was fast and shallow; she was dizzy. 'Did you have that in mind from the first—when you followed me to the cottage?'

Zito's eyes went black. 'All I had in mind was not losing you again. That was the only thing I thought about for those two days.' Again a fleeting guilt shadowed his face. 'On Sunday night when we made love I realised you might become pregnant.' He looked away, then back at her, as if trying to make her understand. 'And yes, I wanted it. I thought—hoped—it was what you wanted too. A pledge of a new beginning.'

Just as Roxane had persuaded herself that at last he had begun to understand why she'd had to distance herself from his overwhelming presence. Deep down, was it possible she also had wanted that ultimate proof of their love, of its permanence and promise—Zito's child?

Zito said, 'I rationalised to myself that you knew what you were doing. In the light of day I knew that not discussing it was—unfair.'

Briefly he shut his eyes and his shoulders hunched. 'I thought maybe it wouldn't matter, after the way you'd loved me the night before. Even after you flew at me for taking over, telling your boss you couldn't come in, I had a forlorn hope you'd get over it and realise I was right.'

'Even if you were, you shouldn't have—'

'I know,' he cut in. 'I know. When you made your way down those stairs and defied me so coolly, made it crystal clear your job and your much-vaunted independence were more important than me—than us, my illusions about what we'd shared the night before died.'

'So you gave up.' She still found that hard to believe.

His mouth tightened. 'Not at once. I was fully determined to wait until you came home and have it out then. But…while I was waiting I looked around the home you'd made for yourself, and remembered how proud you were of what you'd put into it, and of your professional success. You had new friends, new interests, even a new country. You'd walked away from everything I could give you and built yourself a life that had no room for me.' He looked up, away from her, inspecting the ceiling for a moment as though it held something of great interest. Then he sighed. 'I came round to realising I had to accept that was what you wanted, and if you were pregnant…wait for you to tell me.'

'How did you know I would?'

'You wouldn't keep that from me. When you hadn't called after eight weeks I was both greatly relieved and horribly disappointed.'

And then he'd found out she was pregnant after all.

Roxane said, acid in her voice, 'I could have had an abortion, you know.'

He paled, then shook his head. 'No,' he said. 'I know you would never do that.'

How strange that he knew her so well in some ways, and yet had been so obtuse in others.

The following day three large boxes were delivered to the house, addressed to Roxane. The first contained the primrose-trimmed cane bassinet, complete with mattress—Zito must have asked his mother where to find it. The second box was filled with a variety of baby sheets and blankets in shades of yellow and white, and the other revealed a sturdy primrose-painted changing table with shelves and drawers.

Mr. and Mrs. Robinson helped her set them up in a spare bedroom opposite the master suite. Harry fixed a hook in the ceiling and hung a clown mobile that Roxane's mother had bought for the coming baby. When Zito came home Roxane was standing beside the bassinet with a hand-embroidered baby quilt that his own mother had given her just a week ago. Zito's grandmother had made it before he was born.

She looked up over her shoulder when she heard his footsteps in the passageway, and saw him stop in the doorway, jacketless and with his collar open.

She turned and carefully placed the quilt inside the bassinet, tucking it into the sides.

As she straightened, Zito's arms came about her from behind, and she felt his breath stir her hair. She stood very still, prepared for anger, for argument, but he just held her, his hands lightly spread on her belly, his strong body warming her.

Gradually she let herself relax, and without thinking she rested her head back against his shoulder.

'You've been busy,' he said at last. 'I hope you haven't been overdoing it.'

'The Robinsons did all the hard work. They're almost as bad as you at coddling me.'

'Bad?'

'I'm not made of glass.'

His arms tightened fractionally. 'Hardly.'

'You needn't rub it in.'

'Rub what in?'

'That I've grown big and clumsy.'

He turned her round, stepping back a little to survey her. 'Pregnant and beautiful,' he said.

'It's kind of you—'

Zito shook his head vehemently. 'You're more beautiful now than you've ever been—and you always were the loveliest thing I'd ever seen in my life.'

'Zito—' She was shaken, distressed and yet stirred to a kind of sad pride that he still thought so, because the sincerity in his voice was undeniable. 'One day I'll be old.'

His eyes crinkled. 'So will I. And I'll still think the same.'

He spoke as though they would grow old together.

'Zito?'

He caught her hands, holding them loosely. 'Yes, my beautiful wife?'

That gave Roxane her cue. She knew she'd been avoiding this, knew he had too. She braced herself. 'Aren't you…aren't you taking a lot for granted?'

His eyes narrowed. The grip on her hands momentarily became almost painful, then he dropped them. 'For instance?'

Roxane said baldly, 'I haven't promised to stay after the baby's born.'

He couldn't quite hide the shock in his eyes. His face had gone an odd, pasty colour. 'You'd leave your child?'

'No!' Her own eyes widened at that. 'Of course not.'

Zito said loudly, 'I won't allow you to take away my son.'

After a moment of blank disbelief, rage such as she had never known surged through her body until she was shaking with it. She'd thought he was trying to change. The delivery of the baby furniture while Zito was at work seemed to have been a silent message, leaving it to her to decide which room they should be placed in.

But now his true colours were showing again. Disappointment added to her fury. 'You can't stop me!' she fired at him.

'Can't I?' He turned away from her, jamming his hands into his pockets, taking a few swift strides to turn in the doorway as if he'd keep her trapped in the room if necessary. 'If I sued for custody, do you think you'd win?'

Oh, God. Her heart went into a sickening dive.

He'd hire the most high-powered lawyers in Australia, and they'd prove he could afford the best child-care and education.

She couldn't deny that he'd be a loving father, and maybe the court would believe his large, close family could take the place of a deserting wife and solo mother who'd had to give up her job and didn't know where the next mortgage payment was coming from.

'You bastard!' Her hands were clenched, her cheeks burning although her temples were chilled. She wanted to hit him.

Instead she walked, head high, to the doorway and made to brush past him.

Zito didn't move, grabbing at her arm. 'Roxane!' he said hoarsely. There was colour in his face now, a dark line of it running under each cheekbone.

'Let me go!' She defied him with her eyes, not struggling, but her whole body stiffly resistant. 'Or are you going to lock me up and throw away the key?'

'I can't lock you up—I wouldn't.' He held her a moment longer, then with an oddly defeated look, he dropped his hand and stepped aside.

She crossed the passageway and went straight to her dressing room. When Zito came in she was dragging clothes from hangers.

'What are you doing?' His voice was calm, but with an underlying roughness.

Roxane bent, with some difficulty, and thrust a rolled-up skirt into an open suitcase on the floor. 'Packing.' She picked up a pair of sneakers.

'Darling, don't be ridiculous.'

She didn't even think about it. There was no decision, no hesitation. In an instant she straightened and the shoes flew from her hand with all the force of her arm behind them.

One of them hit his shoulder, the other whacked straight into his face, leaving a red welt just below his left eye.

Appalled at herself, she stood perfectly still, unable to move or speak, scarcely even breathing.

Maybe Zito felt the same way. He'd not even had time to dodge until it was too late. Now he stood staring at her as if he'd never seen her before. Which didn't surprise Roxane. She felt like a stranger to herself, someone standing outside her body and watching this whole horrible scene.

Zito spoke first, his voice oddly hoarse. 'Did that make you feel better?'

Momentarily it had. While the adrenalin lasted she'd experienced a fierce, sizzling release of built up emotional tension.

'*Yes!*' she said. And burst into wild, sobbing tears.

Zito stood there a bit longer, seemingly as totally at sea as she was. Then he stepped forward and pulled her into his arms.

Still sobbing, she tried to fight him at first, but when he swept her bulky form up and carried her into the bedroom she gave in.

At her bed he didn't let go, but settled himself beside her on the cover, holding her against him until the crying jag was over, and she lay with her face buried against his shirt, her swollen eyelids tiredly closed.

Even then he didn't move, but she slowly became aware of his breath warming her wet cheek, the rise and fall of his chest against her newly tender breasts, and how he'd curved his body to accommodate the baby within hers. They were so close that he must have felt the tiny movements their son was making. It would be the nearest thing to what she felt herself.

This quiet sharing was almost more intimate than making love. For once she felt absolutely at peace. Some words that had been read at their wedding floated into her mind. *The two shall be one flesh.* At this moment she felt she totally understood them.

Zito's voice rumbled over her head. 'Are you asleep?'

Infinitesimally Roxane shook her head. The movement brought her cheek against bare skin. She opened her eyes and saw his discarded jacket and crumpled tie thrown over the end of the bed.

Into her mind came a clear, disconcerting picture of Zito entering the house, bounding up the stairs, ripping off his tie and unbuttoning the constricting collar of his business shirt as he went, and heading immediately for their bedroom to find out if she'd set up the bassinet in here. And seeing that she hadn't.

And then he'd come looking for her, and simply taken her silently in his arms, accepting that she'd stuck by her avowed intention of moving out of their room after the baby's birth.

One solitary tear squeezed itself from the corner of her eye and ran onto his skin. Unthinkingly, she turned and gathered the salty moisture with her tongue.

Zito's arms tightened, but he lay perfectly still. He said, very quietly, 'I didn't mean any of it. I'm a fool. A total, certified idiot. I thought you'd stay if I did everything right. No pressure, no demands, no bullying. And it seemed to be working…we've been getting on so well, and I hoped you'd decided for the baby's sake you could bear to stay, even if we weren't…if we weren't living like a husband and wife.'

'Would you settle for that?'

'I'll settle for anything if you'll only stay. I never meant to threaten you. That was my temper talking, and fear.'

'Fear?'

'Sheer bloody terror.' His arms tightened. 'Fear of losing you for good, fear that something terrible might happen to you if I'm not there watching you. Fear that you'll never love me again.'

Roxane held her breath, time seeming suspended. Her heart thudded. A scattered jumble of half-thoughts and inexpressible doubts helter-skeltered through her mind.

She felt Zito breathe in deeply, then let it go. 'I always thought,' he said, 'I was a fairly liberated sort of guy. With four sisters, all of them smart and capable and more than willing to straighten me out, how could I be otherwise?'

Easily, Roxane thought. She recalled Serena's remark about his parents' expectation that he'd always look after his younger sisters. And the picture she'd drawn of her parents' and grandparents' marriages. *Nonno and my dad lay down the law and expect their women and children to follow it.* He had absorbed more than he knew of their standards. Protectiveness had run rampant in the Riccioni males. Their women, accustomed to it for generations, had inborn strategies for dealing with it without turning into doormats, but nothing had prepared Roxane. She'd simply had no idea what to do.

Zito continued, 'The first time I laid eyes on you I had this mad urge to carry you off and keep you safe forever.'

'I wasn't in any danger.'

He moved very slightly. She wasn't sure but she thought he'd kissed her hair. 'Only from me. I raced you into marriage, hoping I could hold you with a wedding ring, and determined I would make you so happy you'd never look at anyone else.'

'I never did!'

'But they looked at you. I was insecure enough to worry about that...'

'Insecure? *You?*' She lifted her head away from his chest to stare at him.

'I was your first. What if you tired of me...what if you were curious about how sex would be with someone else?'

Roxane blinked, her eyes stinging. 'I was married to you! Forsaking all others...I didn't need anyone else. Only you.'

'Not the way I needed you.'

He said it with such quiet, intense sincerity she was dumb, not meeting his eyes.

His voice was low and very nearly inaudible. 'I wanted more than anything in the world to protect you from harm, from anything that might hurt you. Every time I held you in my arms, felt the softness of your skin, the way your bones seemed so fragile compared to mine, it scared me. I loved your body, adored it. And I loved your laughter and your eagerness to please not just me but my family, the empathy you had with my sisters, your serenity, and the fact that in so many ways you seemed older than your age.'

The result of being an only child of older parents, she guessed, and being around their friends a lot. She'd always found older people interesting, full of knowledge, and she'd enjoyed learning from them. Maybe it was one reason she'd got on so well with Zito's grandfather.

'But,' Zito continued, 'you had delightful moments of naiveté that reminded me how young you really were.'

Secretly, Roxane made a wry face, but she said nothing.

'They scared me sometimes, although I adored them, in a different way. They laid you open to other kinds of hurt. And you trusted me.' His voice lowered further. 'I was determined you'd never have reason to lose that trust. I wanted you to know you could rely on me to keep you safe and secure, always.'

Roxane sighed. 'I suppose I seemed an ungrateful bitch.'

She felt the slight tremor of his silent laugh. 'You never went up in sparks like my sisters. Or threw shoes.'

Ashamed, she burrowed her face against his shirt. 'I've never thrown anything at anyone before.'

'Maybe you should have.'

'Is that what it takes to get your attention?'

'You've always had my attention. I thought that was your chief complaint.'

'It was just too much. You've never done anything by halves, have you?'

'Serena,' Zito said with difficulty, 'says you felt smothered. That was what you were trying to tell me, before we made this baby?'

Against his chest, Roxane nodded. 'And in the letter you tore up.'

'I shouldn't have done that.'

'It probably didn't make a lot of sense,' she admitted. 'I was too mixed up to put what I was feeling into words.'

'And I was too busy justifying myself and working up a temper to take them in.'

'Justifying yourself?' She glanced up quickly, then down. Her hand moved, playing with a button on his shirt.

'No one likes admitting they've been wrong. The painful, pitiful truth is, you were the centre of my world, and I'd have done anything to remain the centre of yours. I'm sorry, Roxane, for being pigheaded and selfish, and a coward.'

She gave a smothered laugh, raising her head. 'A coward?'

'Too frightened to listen when you were trying to tell me you were unhappy.'

Roxane was listening now, every nerve on the alert. Was he actually saying he'd been wrong?

She felt his jaw move against her temple as he spoke. 'All I could think of was to give you more money, more social life, more…loving. I'm hellishly sorry that I drove you away, and more than sorry I've made you feel trapped all over again. Most of all, I'm sorry for threatening you. Whatever happens after the baby's born will be entirely over to you.' He couldn't quite control the way his voice cracked there. 'Only, whatever you decide, I beg you on my knees, don't shut me out of your life altogether. Yours and our baby's.'

Whatever *she* decided? Roxane pushed away from his chest to study him, trying to be dispassionate, analytical.

He cleared his throat. 'Where are you planning to go?' he asked.

'I thought,' she said, cautiously, 'I'd go to my parents, until the baby comes. There's very little risk now.'

His face was granite, but he nodded jerkily. 'If that's what you want.' He lay rigid and still for a moment, then released her and got off the bed. 'I'll help you pack.'

Astonished, Roxane sat up, then slid off the bed as he made for the dressing room and came back with the case she'd left there.

'What else do you want in here?' He crossed to the drawer where she kept her nightclothes. 'These?'

He held a pair of pyjamas with a long, full top.

Dumbly, Roxane nodded. As if in a trance she went to the dressing table and pulled out bras, panties.

'Will you let me support you financially?' Zito asked, standing beside her as she tucked the undies into the case. 'No strings, I swear.' He cleared his throat again. 'Have you thought about where you'd like to live...eventually? I could get you a house of your own. For the baby's sake,' he added. 'It could even be in his name, if you like. Although you're entitled...'

'Do you mean this?' she asked him, scanning his face.

'Every word.'

'You'd help me,' she pressed, 'after I walked out on you...again?'

He looked as though he was trying to smile but it hurt him too much. 'Don't you get it yet?' he said.

'I would do anything for you—even break my own heart. *Anything.*' He heaved in a breath and said quietly, not looking at her, 'Even if it means letting you go…forever.'

Roxane felt dizzy. She couldn't take her eyes off him, fear and hope and a lingering suspicion all roiling around in hopeless chaos in her heart.

'Thank you,' she said. 'I'll…think it over.'

The skin over the bones of his face seemed to shrink, and as he forced his gaze back to her, his eyes went opaque and expressionless. 'You'll need your toothbrush,' he said.

'Yes.'

'Anything else from the bathroom?'

Roxane tried to think. 'Will you mind if I take the bath oil?'

Already on his way to the bathroom, Zito threw her a remote glance. 'I won't be using it.'

He brought the bottle and her toothbrush and a tube of toothpaste, and she tucked them into a plastic-lined pocket in the suitcase.

Zito looked around, the skin between his eyebrows creased in a frown. 'Anything else?'

She picked up a couple of books from the bedside table and put them in too shaking her head. 'Not right now.'

'You can come and get your other stuff any time.' He closed the lid and snapped shut the clasps. 'You might need a jacket.'

It wasn't cold, but he was already in the dressing room, jerking a cotton jacket from one of the hangers. He held it for her and Roxane slipped her arms into it.

'I'll drive you,' Zito said.

Not looking at her, he swung the case into his hand and started making for the door.

He really meant it. She could tell he hated this, but he was going to let her walk away. Live her own life.

Without him.

'Zito.'

He stopped but didn't turn. 'Forgotten something?'

'Yes, I think so.'

He still had his back to her. It was rigid, his broad shoulders squared, his proud dark head bowed.

She tried twice to get the words past her throat, and finally forced them out. 'I think I'd forgotten how much I love you.'

CHAPTER TWELVE

ZITO turned then, slowly, like an old man. But his eyes blazed. 'Roxane,' he said, 'this is hard enough for me as it is. Don't torture me.'

'I don't want to torture you, Zito. I don't want to leave, either.'

He put down the suitcase but otherwise he didn't move. 'You'd better be sure about this,' he said, sounding as if his throat was raw. 'I don't know if I'm strong enough to go through it again. Next time,' he said huskily, 'I might just manacle you and lock you in the cellar.'

'We don't have a cellar.'

'Damn.'

They stood looking at each other, solemnly despite the desperate lightness of their words. 'I might start throwing shoes again,' she warned him.

'Do,' he invited, 'any time I start being overbearing and...ridiculous.'

'I can't promise that...but I will let you know.'

Zito nodded. 'Okay.'

'Maybe I did want your baby, deep down,' she confessed. 'Maybe that's why I didn't consciously think about it.'

She saw him swallow, but he didn't speak, and she guessed he couldn't, but his eyes were full of hope, desperation...and love.

'Will you...how do you really feel about the baby?' she asked a little anxiously.

Maybe that was a smile she saw in his eyes. 'It's what brought you back to me, however reluctantly. And watching how he's changed your body, the glow in your face when you feel him move inside you…it's been a revelation. I love him already, because he's yours—yours and mine. He and I…we're going to get along just fine.'

'You'll be ganging up on me. Two males with those Riccioni genes.'

'You'll stand up to us.' He started coming toward her.

'I will,' she said, confident now that she could. 'That was the mistake I made, letting you carry on exactly as your father and grandfather did.'

'They had happy marriages.'

'I know.' And it was that pattern that he'd unconsciously followed—naturally, she supposed—while her lack of opposition had encouraged it. Fostered deep down, she supposed, by her fear that he might not keep loving her if she crossed him in any way. 'But times change, and so have I. I'm not your mother or your grandmother.'

His grin this time was real. 'Thank the Lord.'

He put his arms around her again and within minutes they were back on the bed, Roxane's hands were on the buttons of his shirt, and Zito's were…everywhere. On her face, her neck, his thumb brushing her ear, then both hands finding her breasts, gently tracing the full, firm outlines.

When he began undressing her in turn she looked at him hesitantly. 'You haven't seen me naked lately. I'm afraid…you won't like what you see.'

'Don't be…si—shy,' he said. And she smiled,

realising he was watching his words. 'I can't wait to see you.'

And in the next few minutes she discovered a new meaning of the words of the marriage service—*with my body I thee worship*. Because that was what he did, with his eyes, his hands, his mouth, and finally, in the most miraculous, mysterious way of all, when they were as close as any two human beings could be, except for the miracle that was already taking place in her womb.

He tried to be gentle, but in passion they both forgot gentleness. When it was over he touched her swollen lips and looked rueful. 'Did I hurt you?'

'No.' Roxane shook her head against the pillow. She reached up and ran her thumb over the bruise that was colouring under his eye. 'I shouldn't have done that.'

'You could kiss it better.'

She touched her lips to it. 'What will we tell people?'

'That you finally beat me into submission.'

Roxane made a small, scornful sound. 'No one will believe that.'

'What was that you said one time,' Zito commented a few months later, holding his bawling son in his arms in the darkened bedroom, 'about the two of us ganging up on you? Seems to me it's the other way round.'

'I don't remember,' Roxane lied, hastily opening the front of her nightgown. She held out her arms and took the child.

'You are supposed to be resting, not insisting I bring this demanding little monster to you at four in morning. Marina says he might go back to sleep if we leave him for a while.'

'He isn't going back to sleep,' Roxane declared firmly. He'd been in full cry, not just whimpering, when she'd slipped from under the covers before Zito hauled her back and got out of bed himself to fetch the baby to her. 'He's hungry.'

'He's always hungry.'

'He's a big baby, takes after his father. Maybe in a few weeks he'll give up one of his night feeds. Right now he needs it.'

'You know best.' Zito shrugged.

He switched on the night-light and seated himself close to her on the bed, his arm going about her as she sat propped against the pillows. Roberto was sucking contentedly, and Roxane smiled down at him, then turned to share the smile with Zito.

He, too, was looking at their son. He touched the downy dark head with gentle fingers, lifted his eyes to Roxane, and raised his hand to tuck a strand of hair behind her ear. 'You're so beautiful,' he murmured. 'Both of you. I know I should never have done what I did to you, but the truth is I can't be sorry about him.'

'I'm not sorry either,' Roxane acknowledged. In truth, she never had been. Dismayed, fearful, but not sorry.

Roberto hiccuped and gave a protesting cry.

Distracted, Roxane adjusted his position in her arms. 'You shouldn't be so greedy,' she told him sternly.

'We can't help it,' Zito said. 'Neither of us can get enough of you.'

Roxane returned her eyes to the baby, and felt a

piercingly familiar sensation, a strange mixture of joy and terror and heartbreak. 'Is this how you felt about me?' she asked Zito. 'As if it was absolutely necessary to keep me from the slightest hurt, and it was your job to know what I needed and see that I got it, even if I didn't know myself?'

'Yes. Exactly.'

Softly, she said, 'I think I understand.'

'I didn't take into account that you weren't a helpless baby.'

'I'm a mother now. Maybe it helps?'

'Maybe. You were very brave, it was awesome. I've never admired anyone so much in all my life. And you're so competent with him. So sure of yourself.'

'Instinct—and my mother's advice. Your mother's too.'

'Thank you for giving me a second chance.' Zito paused. 'If you still want a job, one of our catering managers is retiring in a few months. I've suggested you might like to give it a try.'

Roxane turned astonished eyes on him. 'What did your father say—and your grandfather?'

'I said you could do it,' he answered, leaving her to guess at their reaction. 'You've got the experience and you're a natural organiser. We could hire a nanny for Roberto, but she'd have to live in because your hours could be irregular. Do you think you could fit the job around his needs if there was someone with him all the time?'

He was taking her breath away. 'You wouldn't mind?'

'Does that matter?' he asked. He slanted her a smile. 'No, I wouldn't mind. But it's your decision.'

Her decision. No question, no subtle pressure. She almost believed he really wouldn't mind. He'd got much more relaxed about things since Roberto's birth. She hadn't objected to him taking charge then—it had been blissful to let him deal with the medical people and the form-filling, reassuring to know that he'd be with her every minute, see she was well cared for and that everything that needed doing would be done, leaving her nothing to worry about but her own body and the baby.

'I'll think about it,' she said.

He turned her to face him again. 'If you don't want to work for the family, say so. It's not a way of keeping you under my eye.'

'I will.' If Zito had been afraid of losing her in the early stages of their marriage, she had been afraid too. Afraid to rock the boat, afraid to argue or assert herself. Now she knew that their relationship could stand up to arguments, to disagreements, even to occasional anger and irrationality. They were strong enough to get through those storms.

'I don't want to take you over,' Zito insisted.

'I know,' she said. 'I love you, but I won't let you ride roughshod over me. I thought you knew that by now.'

'I should,' Zito agreed. He smiled into her eyes. 'You're a sassy woman, Mrs Riccioni. And I love you too.'

He bent his head and kissed her, gently and then quite fiercely, and she kissed him back.

'When that young guy's finished with you,' Zito said, removing his lips from hers for long enough to look down at his son, 'I have a few plans of my own. With your agreement,' he added.

Roxane laughed. 'You have it,' she assured him. 'All the way.'

He kissed her shoulder and settled himself against the pillows behind them, content to wait his turn.

The world's bestselling romance series.

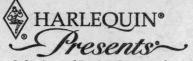

HARLEQUIN® *Presents*

Seduction and Passion Guaranteed!

**We are pleased to announce
Sandra Marton's fantastic new series**

The O'CONNELLS

In order to marry, they've got to gamble on love!

Don't miss...

KEIR O'CONNELL'S MISTRESS

Keir O'Connell knew it was time to leave Las Vegas when he became
consumed with desire for a dancer. The heat of the desert must have
addled his brain! He headed east and set himself up in business—
but thoughts of the dancing girl wouldn't leave his head.
And then one day there she was, Cassie...

**Harlequin Presents #2309
On sale March 2003**

Pick up a Harlequin Presents® novel and you will enter a world
of spine-tingling passion and provocative, tantalizing romance!

Available wherever Harlequin books are sold.

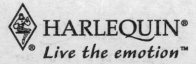

HARLEQUIN®
Live the emotion™

Visit us at www.eHarlequin.com

The world's bestselling romance series.

Seduction and Passion Guaranteed!

They're guaranteed to raise your pulse!

**Meet the most eligible medical men of the world,
in a new series of stories, by popular authors,
that will make your heart race!**

**Whether they're saving lives or dealing with desire,
our doctors have got bedside manners that
send temperatures soaring....**

Coming in Harlequin Presents in 2003:

THE DOCTOR'S SECRET CHILD by Catherine Spencer
#2311, on sale March

THE PASSION TREATMENT by Kim Lawrence
#2330, on sale June

THE DOCTOR'S RUNAWAY BRIDE by Sarah Morgan
#2366, on sale December

**Pick up a Harlequin Presents® novel and you will enter a world
of spine-tingling passion and provocative, tantalizing romance!**

Available wherever Harlequin books are sold.

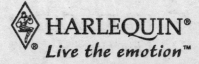

Live the emotion™

Visit us at www.eHarlequin.com

If you enjoyed what you just read,
then we've got an offer you can't resist!

Take 2 bestselling
love stories FREE!
Plus get a FREE surprise gift!

Clip this page and mail it to Harlequin Reader Service®

IN U.S.A.	IN CANADA
3010 Walden Ave.	P.O. Box 609
P.O. Box 1867	Fort Erie, Ontario
Buffalo, N.Y. 14240-1867	L2A 5X3

YES! Please send me 2 free Harlequin Presents® novels and my free surprise gift. After receiving them, if I don't wish to receive anymore, I can return the shipping statement marked cancel. If I don't cancel, I will receive 6 brand-new novels every month, before they're available in stores! In the U.S.A., bill me at the bargain price of $3.57 plus 25¢ shipping & handling per book and applicable sales tax, if any*. In Canada, bill me at the bargain price of $4.24 plus 25¢ shipping & handling per book and applicable taxes**. That's the complete price and a savings of at least 10% off the cover prices—what a great deal! I understand that accepting the 2 free books and gift places me under no obligation ever to buy any books. I can always return a shipment and cancel at any time. Even if I never buy another book from Harlequin, the 2 free books and gift are mine to keep forever.

106 HDN DNTZ
306 HDN DNT2

Name	(PLEASE PRINT)	
Address	Apt.#	
City	State/Prov.	Zip/Postal Code

* Terms and prices subject to change without notice. Sales tax applicable in N.Y.
** Canadian residents will be charged applicable provincial taxes and GST.
  All orders subject to approval. Offer limited to one per household and not valid to
  current Harlequin Presents® subscribers.
  ® are registered trademarks of Harlequin Enterprises Limited.

PRES02   ©2001 Harlequin Enterprises Limited

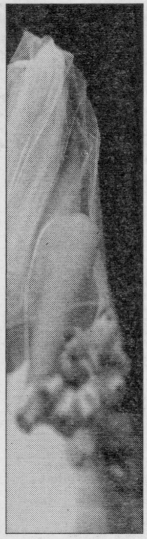

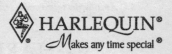

The world's bestselling romance series.

HARLEQUIN®
Presents

Seduction and Passion Guaranteed!

Hot-Blooded Husbands

Let them keep you warm tonight!

**Don't miss the final
part of Michelle Reid's
red-hot series!**

A PASSIONATE MARRIAGE

Greek tycoon Leandros Petronades married
Isobel on the crest of a wild affair. But
within a year the marriage crashed and
burned. Three years later, Leandros wants to
finalize their divorce—or thinks he does.
But face-to-face with Isobel again, he finds
their all-consuming mutual attraction is
as strong as ever....

**Harlequin Presents #2307
On sale March 2003**

**Pick up a Harlequin Presents® novel and you will enter a world
of spine-tingling passion and provocative, tantalizing romance!**

Available wherever Harlequin books are sold.

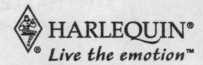

HARLEQUIN®
Live the emotion™

Visit us at www.eHarlequin.com